Scottish S

Selected and edited by
Gordon Jarvie

Oxford University Press

Oxford University Press, Walton Street, Oxford OX2 6DP

Oxford New York Toronto
Delhi Bombay Calcutta Madras Karachi
Petaling Jaya Singapore Hong Kong Tokyo
Nairobi Dar es Salaam Cape Town
Melbourne Auckland

and associated companies in
Berlin Ibadan

Oxford is a trade mark of Oxford University Press

© Oxford University Press 1992

ISBN 0 19 831281 4

Set by Pentacor PLC, High Wycombe, Bucks

Printed in Great Britain

Cover illustration by
Sarah Hopkins

Ro1112

$F_{5/5}$
23.106

Contents

Acknowledgements

The editors and publishers are grateful for permission to include the following copyright stories in this collection.

Keith Aitchison, 'Blood' from *Scottish Short Stories*. (Collins, annual). Copyright Keith Aitchison. **George Mackay Brown**, 'The Tree and the Harp' from *The Masked Fisherman*. Reprinted by permission of John Murray (Publishers) Ltd. **Elspeth Davie**, 'Allergy', reprinted in *Modern Scottish Short Stories*, ed. F. Urquhart & Giles Gordon (Faber, 1978). Copyright Elspeth Davie 1978. Reprinted by permission of Sheil Land Associates. **Douglas Dunn**, 'The Stonethrower'. Copyright Douglas Dunn. **George Friel**, 'Her Brother Died', first published in *New Stories*, Feb/Mar 1936. Reprinted by permission of Brian Elliot. **Alasdair Gray**, 'The Star' reprinted in *Unlikely Stories Mostly* (Canongate Publishing, 1982). Copyright Alasdair Gray. **Robin Jenkins**, 'Exile', first published in The Scottish Review, no. 5, Winter 1976. Copyright Robin Jenkins 1976. **Brian McCabe**, 'Kreativ Riting' from I Can Sing, Dance, Rollerskate & Other Stories (Collins). Copyright Brian McCabe. **Bernard MacLaverty**, 'A Time to Dance' from *A Time to Dance and Other Stories*. Reprinted by permission of Jonathan Cape as publishers. **Naomi Mitchison**, 'Remember Me' from *What Do You Think Yourself?* (Paul Harris, 1982). Reprinted by permission of David Higham Associates. **Wilma Murray**, 'Old Wives' Tales' from *Original Prints* Vol. II (1987). Reprinted by permission of Polygon. **Christopher Rush**, 'Tutti Frutti' from *Into the Ebb* (1989). Reprinted by permission of Aberdeen University Press. **Betsy Whyte**, from the opening two episodes of Betsy Whyte's *The Yellow on the Broom*, an autobiography of her early days as a travelling woman (Futura Publications Ltd). Reprinted by permission of Peter R. Cooke, Agent to the Estate of Betsy Whyte.

Every effort has been made to secure all permissions prior to publication. However in a few instances this has not been possible. If contacted the publisher will be pleased to rectify any errors or omissions at the earliest opportunity.

Preface

A fund of good literature is central to any English course, and in a televisual age of limited attention span, the short story form has a special appeal and relevance. Short stories have the enormous advantage that they can be read at a sitting – for homework, or in a forty-minute period – or in the time it takes you to plug in to the latest excerpt of your favourite TV soap.

I believe these are all good stories and that they will have wide appeal. But having said that, I believe also that there is a particular need for a collection of this sort within Scotland. Scottish culture is not generally perceived to be a minority culture by the 'ethnic lobby': but it is a minority culture nonetheless, and as a result serious Scottish writing can experience great difficulty finding commercial outlets. So this book tries to fill a gap for Scottish readers in particular, and it is hoped that they will meet here special echoes of their own society and environment.

A collection like this is of course constrained by considerations of length. It contains thirteen stories, but it might easily have been twice as long. The oldest story – by George Friel – dates to 1936. All the others have been written in the last thirty years, so this is essentially a *modern* collection. I was keen to reflect the sheer *variety* of Scottish writing, so several good stories were set aside because they too nearly resembled others that had already been selected. I wanted dialect, and an echo of the oral tradition: hence *The Yellow on the Broom*. I wanted something of the supernatural: hence the George Mackay Brown story. I wanted a monologue or stream-of-consciousness item: hence *Old Wives' Tales*. I wanted humour: hence *Allergy* and *Kreativ Riting*. And so on. Town and country. Glasgow and Edinburgh. Male and female. Dialect and Standard English. And always I was looking for material that hadn't already featured in too many other books, and trying to produce a collection that amounted to more than the sum of its parts.

Readers will judge the success of these efforts. I hope you will enjoy *all* these stories, and find them stimulating and insightful. Bibliographies at the back of the book list other titles by the writers included in this collection, plus a few who are not. In the section that follows the stories you will find a range of activity material of a sort that will help students focus on the likely demands of the new exams at 16+, including suggestions for pair work, group work, discussion, role play, and written assignments linked to each story. These are however designed as much for purposes of extension and enrichment as to anticipate the demands of Standard Grade and GCSE students. So they should not be worked through mechanically. There is also cross-referencing through the anthology to supplement specific story-based activities and to encourage students to compare different styles and approaches.

Blood

Keith Aitchison

It was a sunny week in late August, when the heat curled along the streets and up the tenement stairs of the baker's oven of a city, that Timothy Maguire came to stay with his widowed sister and his nephew.

'By God, have I not brought the good weather with me!' he exclaimed, putting down his suitcase and beaming at them, his round face shining with sweat.

'Mary!' he embraced his sister, then thrust out his hand. 'And this hulking giant cannot be young Martin?'

'I'm nineteen, Uncle Tim.' Martin's hand was gripped.

'Nineteen, is it?' Timothy whistled. 'By God, there's time passed, and a lot of Maguire grown in this lad, Mary. Does he not look like our father when young?'

'He has the eyes, just. The face is his own father's. Come, sit down.'

Timothy sat and pulled out a handkerchief to mop his face and the wet, darkened roots of his fair hair. 'And how is it with you both?' he asked.

'Martin grows up, and I grow older,' said Mary, and plucked at a lock of her hair. 'Do you see the grey?'

'No more than before.'

'That was four years ago. The funeral.'

'Ah, I meant to come sooner. But business, and other things. You should have come to me for a time.'

'I don't think Belfast is the place for holidays now.'

'Maybe not. It's remarkable how you get accustomed to it all, though,' Timothy paused. 'And it's not as if the cause were not just.'

'The cause!' Mary shook her head. 'You're the son of your father, right enough.'

'And proud of it,' Timothy smiled. 'Was he not a great man after all?'

'What cause?' Martin interjected, curious.

'You don't know?' Timothy stared in amazement, round eyes in a round face.

'That's enough.' Mary rose sharply, and Timothy thought that right enough the years and the widowing had taken more from her than she deserved to lose.

'What cause?' asked Martin once more. 'Ireland?'

'Ireland! Of course, Ireland,' said Timothy with relief. 'Thank God you've not lost your heritage entirely.'

'Half his heritage, or more likely, remembering mother's opinions, one quarter,' said Mary, going into the scullery and speaking back over her shoulder. 'And remember his father, and his side of the family.'

'Aren't they Irish too, with the name O'Brien?' asked Timothy.

'No one remembers when they came over, but it was long ago. And it's near tea-time.'

'The blood's the same. The years don't change it.'

'Ah, the old blood, who knows who else has got into it over the centuries,' said Mary sourly, 'and bugger the old blood for any argument.'

Martin's jaw dropped at the flaring of his mother's temper. Timothy winked at him and gave a long whistle.

'The language!' he called. 'That's my mother's daughter right enough.'

'Who else would put up with you?' Mary asked back, but her voice was no longer sour.

'Do you remember the time mother lost her temper with that butcher in Foyle Street, the one who sold her the wormy meat?'

They laughed together, good humour restored, and Timothy went to his suitcase and brought out a bottle of Irish whiskey.

'Just an aperitif, as the French say.' He poured three glasses. 'It's a great pity James is not still with us, he loved a good whiskey.'

'He never refused any whiskey, good or bad,' said Mary, with neither malice nor sadness, turning her head to smile at Martin and show she was not serious.

'Well now, Martin.' Timothy watched approvingly as his nephew swallowed the whiskey. 'I'll be looking to you to show me around Glasgow. I don't know it at all.'

'You'll have an advantage then,' said Mary. 'Most who do know it well have had to forget the half of what they know in order to find out where they are.'

'Redevelopment?'

'That's the name they give it, the smart name so that we won't notice the way they've ruined the city.'

'The progress is a great thing for them as makes money from it.'

Martin listened to them talk, hearing them drift back down the years to their shared memories. The talk, the memories and the unaccustomed whiskey had softened the Glasgow in his mother's voice. The more she spoke, the more an underlying Belfast edge cut through in the words, as if an echo from the past.

'Tell me, how's young Mary and her man?' asked Timothy suddenly. 'Do you hear from them at all?'

'I do. They're both well, down there in Leeds, and I'm to visit in October and see their new house.'

'New house?' Timothy whistled. 'They must be doing well. And you, young Martin, are you going to visit your sister?'

'No,' said Martin. 'I hope to have found work by then, or else I'll still be looking for it.'

After they had eaten, and after Timothy had remarked that Mary's cooking was still the best east of home, he followed Martin back down the winding stairs and out into the evening, with the tenement shadow sweeping down in a cooling tide along the length of the street, still pleasantly warm for a stroll in shirt-sleeves, with the children calling and playing around the closemouths of the grey tenements curving towards the heart of the city.

Timothy and Martin strolled along the pavement to the main road, and watched the pedestrians and traffic, the city's people in sunlit evening hours between their day and sleep. The doors of the pubs were opened to any cooling breeze, and the sounds of talk and laughter, the clinking of glasses and bottles breathed out on to the pavements in a warm beery invitation.

'When I was in France,' said Timothy, 'the pubs would have tables on the street, where you could sit on evenings like this and take a cool glass. It's a pity we couldn't do that tonight.'

'We haven't the weather for it,' said Martin apologetically. 'It's not like this very often.'

'Still, it would make a great sight, would it not? The Glasgow topers sitting in the rain outside every pub, with their glasses filling up with water and the waiters in mackintoshes and Wellington boots. People would pay to see that.'

Martin laughed, beginning to warm to his uncle's humour.

'And no soldiers,' Timothy mused, watching a group of young men pass by joking among themselves. 'You don't know how lucky you are, Martin. No soldiers, and nobody afraid.'

'I see it on the television,' said Martin, awkward with the sudden change.

'Your television is censored, I'll tell you that. They don't dare to show you even one half of what the soldiers do, over there.'

Martin shuffled his feet, uncomfortable with this grim note in Timothy.

'Ah well,' Timothy slapped Martin's back. 'Why talk of that now? Your lives aren't touched by it, thank God, and I'm on holiday.'

'And do you see,' he continued, 'how the pubs in this street are positively entreating us to cross their thresholds. Are you a drinking man, now?'

'I take a pint or two,' admitted Martin.

'And two it will be,' said Timothy, and steered his nephew into the nearest pub.

A pint in his fist, Timothy took a long pull and smacked his lips. He looked around the pub with a seasoned eye, noting the long formica bar with plain mirrors behind and the gantries on either side. There were little tables in the corners, and over it all a cloud of cigarette smoke and the hard language of men drinking with no women in the company.

4

'A man's pub,' Timothy observed. 'You wouldn't be bringing your girlfriends here, Martin?'

'I haven't got one, just now.'

'Now? Playing the field, is it?'

'Playing nothing. I've no work, Uncle Tim,' Martin felt ashamed, knowing there was no cause for shame. 'No money, no girlfriend.'

'Just "Tim", eh? I'm your mother's younger brother,' Timothy said, and sighed. 'So, no work and no girl. That's hard. And you'll need the job to get the money to find a girl.'

'I had work. But they laid us off, and it's been the dole for three months.'

'Ah, it's hard. I've been without work myself so I know. I do joinery now, my own boss and it keeps me going.'

Timothy looked around the bar, and the smile returned to his face.

'How do you spend your time?' he asked. 'Do you watch the football?'

'The Celtic.' Martin's chin lifted. 'I go to Parkhead with my mates in the season, when we've got the money. We can't afford the away matches.'

'And tell me, is there that powerful atmosphere we hear about? Songs and the Irish flag waving?'

'Songs and chants,' Martin flushed with the alcohol's gift of enthusiasm. 'When we play Rangers, we do it all specially to annoy the Orangemen. We sing the Soldiers' Song and chant "IRA – all the way!" and all that! It's great!'

'Is it now?' Timothy laughed and emptied his glass. 'Well, that sounds like the sons of Erin to me.'

He stood up to make his way to the bar, counting out money into his hand. Martin started to rise, reaching for the pound notes in his hip pocket.

'I'll get this one.'

'You will not,' Timothy reached out with a work-hardened hand and held him down in his seat. 'These are on me, and no arguments.'

It seemed to Martin as if for once a week passed too quickly.

He spent his days and evenings with Timothy. Once they took the train to Edinburgh, together with Mary, and on another day, a glaring hot day, the three of them went down to Largs and passed the day in sunshine on the sand and in the water. That evening, Timothy took them for dinner in a white-fronted restaurant with ropes looped ship-fashion around the balcony rails, and they ate and drank royally at a white-clothed table looking out at the sea and the hills of Arran.

It seemed to Martin that Timothy had lifted him from the grey drudgery of unemployment, and it was a feeling of gratitude, together with his natural liking for his uncle, that brought them as close and familiar as any friends.

A question of his grandfather began to build in Martin's mind. He had never known him, and somehow the subject had never arisen at home, or perhaps it had been deliberately avoided. As the week passed, with Timothy's presence the vacuum of his mother's Irish family began to fill in patches, like clouds gathering in a clear sky, and subtly altered the way in which Martin saw himself. He remembered Timothy speaking: 'A great man after all,' and curiosity nagged at him with the persistence of toothache, now sharp and demanding, now dull and weak, but always unavoidably claiming his attention, and refusing quiescence.

The night before Timothy left for home, the pair of them travelled to a famously Irish bar on the south side of the city. The evening began to a medley of soft Irish songs played and sung by a blackbrowed accordionist, and later, as the drink flowed both into him and into his audience, and the clouds of cigarette smoke streamed up through the evening to the yellow ceiling, the soft lilts of the Gael gradually made way for the harsher war songs and proud laments of the Fenian men and the IRA. Timothy sang with others in the bar, a mellow baritone in *Sean South*, and even *The Belfast Brigade*, and Martin listened and drank among the other descendants of expatriate Irish, and was swept along on their hazy tides of emotion.

'Tell me about grandfather,' he asked Timothy. 'You said I resemble him.'

Timothy leaned back in his chair and looked at Martin, raising and dropping his eyebrows, crinkling and smoothing his forehead. He sucked the air in through his teeth with a hiss, and expelled it again.

'You don't know,' he said finally. 'Your mother has no regard for him at all; I think she'd be angry if I spoke much of him.'

'Tell me,' Martin's appetite was whetted. 'Tell me! I'll keep quiet, I won't let on anything you say.'

'It's your right to know, maybe,' mused Timothy. 'It's a man's birthright to know the ways of his family. But it's not for me to be telling you. You're your mother's son, not mine.'

'Please!' Martin begged, frantic with drink and curiosity. 'You've got to tell me, can't you see?'

Timothy tapped his glass and listened to the accordionist play a lament for Cathal Brugha. He nodded slowly.

'I will, then. If you don't blab.'

'I won't!'

'It'll be our secret, yes? Between us only?'

'I promise, I promise!' Martin said eagerly.

'Very well,' Timothy spoke quietly, beneath the music's insistent notes. 'Your grandfather, my father, Sean Maguire, fought and died for Ireland. The Brits shot him down on a hillside in Fermanagh, and he lies with the heroes in the Republican plot in Armagh.'

Martin felt the impact of each word, opening and shutting his mouth in amazement. He stared silently at Timothy's serious round face, and knew that this was the truth. His world turned upon itself.

'I never knew,' he managed at last. 'I was never told. Never!'

'Your grandmother had a hard time bringing up us children without a man to provide. She never really forgave father for putting country before family.'

Timothy shrugged, fatalistic at the unchanging strangeness of things.

'You see, Martin,' he continued, 'that's the way women think, that's how they're made. The bitterness rubbed off on Mary, and that's how you never were told at all, I suppose.'

'She should have told me,' Martin said, a note of anger in his voice.

'It's a secret, mind,' Timothy said sharply, a little alarmed. 'Not a word!'

'I promised,' agreed Martin, and began to fill with more questions.

They drank more than on any other night spent together in a bar. Irish whiskey with every pint, and a pint in every half-hour, downed to the note of the accordion and the singing.

Towards closing time, a small old man in a dark jacket walked among the patrons in the bar, carrying an unmarked collecting can. He stepped up to Timothy and shook the can gently, so that the coins chinked and clashed inside like bullets dropping into a magazine.

'For the boys,' he said with a wink and a grin. 'For the lads and the great cause. Come on now, dig into your pockets.'

Timothy looked benevolently at the small man and winked drunkenly back at him.

'Sure,' he said in his own Belfast voice, quietly, so as not to slur the words. 'Sure, am I not one of the boys myself?'

'Belfast?' The small man asked, stiffening with sudden respect. 'Are you one of the lads in Belfast then?'

'I am,' said Timothy, 'I am, but I'll say nothing more. You understand.'

He reached and gripped the small man's arm.

'Tell nobody,' he gave another drunken conspiratorial wink.

'God's blessing on you, let me shake that hand,' said the small man fervently. 'God keep you safe and strengthen your arm!'

Martin watched and heard all of this, his mouth opening once more in amazement. He was already in an alcoholic fog, and excitement pumped at his heart, catching at his breath. The small man left, and Timothy looked into his empty glass with a little smile.

'Tim,' said Martin in a hushed voice, 'Tim, are you – ?'

' – I'll say nothing,' said Timothy, but smiled fondly at him. 'And you'll say nothing, either. It's the only way, Martin. The only way.'

He left next day, producing like a conjuror a bottle of perfume from his pocket for Mary. Martin he left with a crackling envelope, and a smiling warning to a wagging finger.

'Don't be opening that till I've gone now, you hear?'

He waved back through the taxi window, and was gone. Martin thought that the tenement flat seemed both empty and smaller without Timothy. Even the six crisp five-pound notes in the envelope could not fill an empty chair, and he did not hear his mother when she said with a shaking of the head: 'He's some talker, that Timothy. A great tale-spinner, he could make a living at it.'

There was a change in Martin, it seemed to Mary. He began to go regularly to mass, even to the men's club in the chapel hall on a Friday night, and Mary was pleased to see him taking his religion more seriously. That was her thought, and wrong.

Martin's interest was not religious. It was Ireland that filled his soul, not God. He listened to the Irish priest, Father O'Cahan, and revelled in the soft brogue and gentle country homilies which studded the old man's ceremony. On Friday nights in the club the talk would turn to the old days in Ireland, days that had become rosier and more entrancing as the years sped from them and they sank back into old men's tales of their youth or of their fathers' day.

Martin listened and was no longer only another unemployed youth. He knew himself to be an exiled child of Ireland, one of the wild geese in a foreign land awaiting the day of return. The older men knew that they would not return, and indeed most had no wish to leave Scotland, but Martin, in the flush of youthful discovery, began to believe that this Ireland of the past lived still, that this Ireland of the cottages and the colleens and the heroes still awaited her exiled children from across the dividing sea.

Martin kept this from his mother, another secret, and a shadow of the secrets he had shared with Timothy. So it was that when the week came which she was to spend in Leeds with her daughter, Mary had no more than the usual mother's doubts as to the wisdom of leaving her son on his own.

She was packed, ready and on the train, and looked again at Martin through the open window of the door.

'Are you sure, you'll be all right?'

'I'll be fine, Mum,' Martin hid his impatience at his mother's solicitude. 'I'm twenty next month. I'll be fine.'

'You've got enough money. Remember the paper money,' she raised her voice as the whistle blew shrill along the platform. 'Don't keep that cold pork after tomorrow.'

She leaned awkwardly through the window and Martin kissed her rouged cheek as the train began to move slowly beneath the high glass and iron roof towards the gleaming rails beyond.

'And don't get up to any mischief!' Mary called back.

'I won't, Mum,' Martin waved and stepped back as the train began to bend away from him along the curve of the rail.

'Goodbye, goodbye!' He called and waved, entirely alone for the first time in his life, already tasting the freedom and the pain.

It rained later, long and heavy, the drops sliding like translucent worms across the windows. Martin lifted his eyes above the grey tenements towards the west.

West Belfast was quiet, the storm-lashing rain driving down the stink of the last night's burnings and tear gas. The army had cleared away the fire-blackened debris of cars and lorries hijacked to barricade and burn, and the streets between the rows of terraced houses were wet and cold, with a litter of broken bricks and glass lying here and there to sign the battlegrounds.

The ink ran in blue smudges down the paper when he looked at the scribbled directions. The rain ran straight down the side of the bag and darkened his jeans where they touched.

Martin clutched his anorak tighter at the throat, and picked his way among the jagged fragments of glass beneath a gable end which proclaimed, in foot-high lettering against a background of orange, white and green: 'BRITS OUT! UP THE REPUB-LIC!'

He was almost alone on the street; only a few hurrying souls besides himself braved the torrent from the skies, but behind windows, shadows behind net curtains or in shadows aside from the direct light through the panes, Martin caught glimpses of the motionless watchers who saw him pass.

Dungarvel Street was on the other side of a sudden ugly wasteland of red ash. Martin started across the emptiness, around pools of dark-stained rainwater and past forlorn banks of struggling weeds. A patrol of eight soldiers came sharply along the terrace on the farther side, and Martin told himself that these were the oppressors of his countrymen, but strangely, the words would not take in his mind, and all he really felt was something like disbelief at the sight of these silent running men, dressed in drab green and brown combat gear, and holding ungainly black rifles across their chests. The last two soldiers watched only to the rear, doubling back behind each other to drop and crouch in doorways. As Martin crossed into Dungarvel Street he looked at their white, dirt-streaked faces and saw, with a quickening of disbelief, that a black and dripping rifle muzzle pointed straight at him, and followed his footsteps until the corner took him from its sights.

Martin walked briskly down the street, the tremors in his stomach subsiding, but now even more eager to get indoors and out of the rain. He knocked on Timothy's door. No answer. He knocked again, harder. Again no answer, and with mounting frustration, realizing that Timothy must be out working, he stepped back from the door, glancing up and down the street, turning his head so that the eager rain found its way down inside his collar. From the edge of his vision he saw a corner of the curtain twitch in the neighbour window.

He knocked on that door, twice, before he heard a reluctant voice, an old woman's voice from deep within the hallway.

'Who's that?' The words were quiet as if whispered in the hope that they would not be heard.

'I'm Timothy Maguire's nephew, Martin. He's not in the house, do you know where he'll be?'

'His nephew, do you say?' Frail and suspicious words.

'Yes! Do you know where he is?'

'You might be a nephew, but you're not from here.'

'I'm from Glasgow!' Martin almost shouted with frustration.

11

'His sister's son, Martin O'Brien!'

'Glasgow.' The old voice hesitated, and relented only a little. 'He'll be working. He's never home before five.'

Martin turned back into the rain and retraced his steps down the street and across the empty waste to a pub he had passed on a corner. Screens of thick wire mesh stretched across the windows like stiff grey nets, with crisp bags and scraps of dirty newspaper caught between the wire and the unwashed glass. The door was narrow and heavy, pitted and scarred like a target.

Inside, the pub was dark, dark and silent, the dim afternoon's light seeping weakly through the windows, and the half-dozen men staring wordlessly at Martin. He pushed back the hood of his anorak, and the rain rolled down his shoulders to the floor, emphasizing the silence with the pattering of the drops breaking upon the floor. The barman raised his eyebrows interrogatively as Martin stepped up to the bar.

'Pint of heavy, please,' Martin put his bag on the floor and when there were no words of response, he added, 'Terrible wet today.'

'It is,' the barman passed him the full pint glass and held out his hand.

Martin paid, and drank, turning to lean on the bartop. He could see the other men watching him, and he tried a friendly smile and a nod, and the men looked unsmilingly back at him, and then stirred. One, balding and middle-aged in a donkey jacket, walked around Martin and stood at his elbow, between him and the door. Another, younger, perhaps in his late twenties, stroked back his wet black hair and came to lean on the bar in front of Martin, looking him up and down with a thoughtful pursing of his mouth. Martin caught his dark eyes for an instant, and felt uneasy as those eyes slid away across his face and down his length, finally studying the bag at his feet. The young man lifted his head, and looked steadily at Martin.

'Come far?' He had a soft, almost sleepy voice.

'From Glasgow,' Martin replied, then quickly, 'to see my uncle, Timothy Maguire, Dungarvel Street.'

'I thought I recognized the accent. You'll be Scottish, then?'

'I'm Irish by blood. O'Brien. Timothy's my mother's brother.'

'Common enough names, O'Brien and Maguire. But you sound Scottish to me.'

Martin thought he heard a hard edge pushing into the soft voice; a hard edge, a hint of menace, turning towards threat. He could almost feel the man behind staring at him. He began to feel afraid, and swallowed a gulp of beer to steal seconds in which to mask his fear.

'Born and brought up in Glasgow, I suppose I do,' he said at last, and was glad to hear his voice did not tremble.

He lifted his glass and began to drink hastily, to finish and leave. The young man put a hand on his arm.

'Take your time,' he said easily. 'Aren't we just having a wee talk?'

'I'm off to see my uncle.' Martin put down his glass.

'Timothy Maguire? Well, what's a name after all? And this place is thick with the Maguires.'

'What do you mean?' demanded Martin, talking braver than he felt.

'You could pick any name from a phone book, could you not?'

'Look,' Martin bent to pick up his bag. 'I'm over to see my uncle, and I'm going now.'

'You're not,' and the young man gave a slight nod.

The balding man gripped Martin by the arms, and the young man casually gripped his right wrist and turned it outwards, so that his fingers loosened on the handle, and let the bag fall. Martin cursed and struggled, and the balding man slammed him hard against the bar, twice, winding him. He gasped for breath, blinking back tears of pain, and watched his belongings being impatiently scattered on to the bartop. Finally, the young man held the bag upside down and shook it, then let it fall to the floor.

'Nothing,' he said, and looked at Martin. 'Not a thing. Maybe it's the truth.'

'Take no chances, Michael,' said the balding man.

'Do I ever?' asked the young man irritably, and turned to the other men. 'Patrick, keep a look-out. Sean, find this Timothy Maguire, and bring him.'

The men left. Michael studied Martin again and jerked his head towards a corner with a small rickety table and two chairs.

'Put him over there, Peter. Back towards the door.'

Martin was pushed down sharply into the chair. His ribs ached and he touched them gingerly. He was afraid now, thoroughly afraid.

'What's going on?' he asked, speaking in short gasps, catching at his breath. 'What do you want with me?'

'Indeed,' said Michael, and sat opposite him, 'and that's the whole point – what's going on. This is Ireland. There's a war going on, and you fit the wrong way for us to be happy about you strolling in here and chatting about the weather.'

The barman stuffed Martin's clothes back into the bag, and set it on the bartop.

Michael ticked off his fingers in a casual, unexcited manner, like a teacher making something very plain.

'You're Scottish. You've short hair. You're what – twenty, nineteen?'

'Nineteen,' Martin's mouth trembled and he quickly wiped his hand across it to cover his fear.

'Well, all that means one thing only to me.' Michael leaned forward as if to confide. 'Spy. Soldier. Spy!'

'My name's O'Brien! I'm a Catholic!'

'There's plenty Scottish soldiers with Irish names go to mass. And I don't even know your name is O'Brien, now do I?'

'My uncle will tell you!' Martin said quickly. 'Christ, he's one of the lads himself!'

'One of the lads?' mused Michael. 'A brave freedom fighter is he? Well, well.'

The balding man put a hand on Martin's shoulder and squeezed hard, digging his fingers into the sinews behind the collar bone.

'Do we interrogate him?' he said to Michael.

'You're that eager, Peter,' Michael sighed and sat back in the squeaking wooden chair. 'He could be telling us the truth. Well, part of the truth.'

'In which case we'll know,' said the balding man, 'and there could still be time for the other business.'

He took out a cigarette and lit it, drew deeply and then took the cigarette from his mouth and blew on the coal so that it burned redly. He looked at Michael.

'I don't think so,' said Michael. 'Use it to give yourself cancer instead.'

Peter laughed and drew in a breath of smoke. After a little while he gripped Martin's shoulder once more, and dug his fingers even harder, searching for the pain centres. Martin stood it for a short while, then the hard fingers sent an agonizing spasm through his shoulder and arm. He twisted away and reached up to massage his shoulder.

'Did that hurt?' asked Peter.

'Yes.' Martin felt hatred coming behind the fear.

'Well that's a little indication,' said Peter. 'If you're not what you say you are, that pain will be like a nothing.'

'Leave him alone,' said Michael sharply. 'Violence is a tool, not a pleasure.'

'God, Michael,' Peter grinned maliciously. 'Aren't you becoming the intellectual?'

'You shut up,' said Michael. 'Do you hear me? Shut up!'

Martin listened, and the Ireland of the tales suffocated and died inside him.

Timothy came at last, dressed in his overalls, his face pale and sweating and trying to smile. Michael looked him up and down thoughtfully, as he had earlier inspected Martin.

'Well,' he said finally. 'I know you, Maguire, and you know me. You're no danger to us, or to the enemy. Who's this boy?'

'My nephew, Martin.' Timothy was subdued.

'I'm not sure, Maguire, and I don't take chances. He looks like one of those bloody-minded Scots soldiers to me.'

'He's only a boy!' Timothy took a pace forward.

'I've got boys of his age dying out there,' said Michael evenly, 'and so have the Brits.'

He stood up and walked to stand only a foot away from Timothy, looking levelly into his eyes. Martin saw Timothy turn even paler and look away, down at the floor, shuffling his feet a little.

'Your nephew is under the impression, Maguire, that you're a bold Fenian man, a freedom fighter, one of the lads.'

'Him?' Peter laughed. 'The most he could fight would be a full glass.'

'No, no, a mistake!' Timothy licked his lips. 'I've the greatest respect for you, and I pay my contributions with the best, but I'd never claim your glory for myself! No, never!'

'I should hope you would not,' said Michael, and his eyes did not move from Timothy's face. 'I'm fighting a revolutionary war, and there's enough trouble for us all, without the need to enforce discipline on such as you.'

He put a hand into his jacket pocket, and brought out a blue steel revolver. Timothy stiffened, licking his lips again. Martin could almost feel his fear; almost smell his terror. Michael tapped Timothy on the elbow with the revolver barrel.

'You take my meaning?' he asked, and put the gun back in his pocket.

Timothy nodded, making small stuttering noises, blinking rapidly.

'Like I said,' Michael continued, 'I'm fighting a revolutionary war, and you've never even thrown a bloody brick, let alone been on active service!'

'My father died for Ireland!' said Timothy hoarsely.

'Sure,' said Michael with contempt. 'Is that not your style? Another man's deeds again!'

'I'll make it up to you for your trouble, I will!'

'Oh, you will,' agreed Michael. 'You'll be hearing from us. Now, get out, the pair of you.'

Martin stood up, and Peter tossed his bag at him, hard, using both hands, as if throwing a medicine ball.

'You're a lucky boy. Michael's getting soft!'

'Enough of that!' Michael rounded on him. 'Save your criticisms for the proper time, not here!'

He turned back to Timothy and Martin, still standing without moving.

'I said, get out!' And he turned to the bar and unbidden the barman placed a pint in his hand.

Timothy and Martin walked awkwardly down the street, silence between them. The rain had stopped, and grey clouds swept overhead like tattered banners.

'Come on, we'll go up to the house,' said Timothy at last.

'No,' said Martin. 'I don't want to stay, not after that.'

'They won't trouble you again, Martin,' Timothy spread his hands, 'don't judge us by that!'

'Us?' Martin sneered, and stopped walking, to look at his uncle. 'Us? What's this "us"? You've never thrown a brick, remember?'

A car drove past with the slow speed of a hearse, the passenger gazing out the side window at them. Martin wondered what work they were engaged upon.

'If I'd known you were coming!' Timothy pleaded. 'Martin, you must see, you just got in the way.'

'Do you never wonder who else "just got in the way"? Is that how the cause is won?'

'Martin, Martin! You're upset, and I don't blame you. Come on up to the house, at least for the night, and I'll drive you to Larne tomorrow.'

'No, I'm going,' Martin looked up and down the street for the way out of the terraces and back to the railway station.

'Martin, please. Don't let us part like this.'

Martin looked stiffly past, and Timothy sighed and looked down at his shoes and the wet pavement. There was silver creeping into his hair, and a thinning begun at the crown of his head. Martin felt a new emotion: pity.

'Well, just for tonight, then,' he said, and saw Timothy lift his head and smile a growing shadow of his old beaming smile.

That evening, while Timothy cooked, whistling with his jauntiness mostly restored by a large whiskey, Martin looked out the window at the huddled row of terraced houses opposite, on the other side of the twilight street. A puddle caught the light from the window in a lonely splash of illumination, and he thought with longing of tall grey tenements in the rain.

Kreativ Riting

Brian McCabe

'Today, we are going to do some writing,' said PK. 'Some *creative* writing. You do know what I mean by *creative*, Joe, don't you?' he said to me.

'Eh . . . is that like when ye use they fancy letters and that?' I said.

'No, Joe, it is not. Creative writing has nothing whatsoever to do with they fancy letters and that,' said PK. So I made the face, like Neanderthal Man, and went, 'UHHH.'

We call him PK 'cause his name is Pitcairn, and he is a nut. So anyway, he goes round and gave everybody a new jotter each.

'For God's sake now,' says PK, 'try and use a bit of imagination!' Then he stops at my desk and looks at me and says, 'If you've got one, I mean. You have got an imagination, Joe, haven't you?'

This is him slaggin' me, ken?

So I says, 'Naw, sir, but I've got a video.'

That got a laugh, ken?

So then PK says, 'The only trouble with you, Joe, is your head is choc-a-bloc with those videos and those video nasties. Those video nasties are worse than anything for your brain, Joe.'

Then Lenny Turnbull, who sits behind me and who is a poser, says: 'What brain? Joe's no got a brain in there, sir, just a bitty fresh air between his lugs!'

That got a laugh, ken?

So I turned round and gave Lenny Turnbull a boot in the leg, then he karati-chopped me in the neck, so I slapped him across his puss for him.

PK went spare, ken.

Except, naebody took any notice, so he kept on shouting: 'That's *enough* of that! Come on now 4F, let's have a bit of order round here!'

So then I says, 'Sir, they video nasties is no as bad as glue is for your brain but, is it?'

That got a laugh, ken.

Then Lenny Turnbull who is a poser says, 'Joe's got brain damage, sir, through sniffin' too much glue!'

'Glue sniffing . . . solvent abuse is no laughing matter, let's have a bit of *order round here*! Right. I'm going to get you all to do a piece of writing. You've got a whole two periods to do it in, and what I'd like all of you to do is empty your mind. In your case, Joe,' he said to me, 'that shouldn't be too difficult.'

This is PK slaggin' me again, ken.

So I says, for a laugh, ken: 'How no, sir? I thought you said my mind was choc-a-bloc with video nasties?'

That got a great laugh, ken.

So then PK says, 'That's right, Joe, and what I want you to do is just empty all that junk out of your mind, so that your mind is completely blank, so that you've got a blank page in your mind, just like the one in your jotter. Understand?'

'But sir, this jotter's not blank – it's got lines in it,' I says.

Then PK says: 'Joe, your head probably has lines in it too, through watching all those video nasties.'

Everybody laughed at that, so I did the face like Neanderthal Man again and started hitting my skull with my fist.

'UHHH! UHHH!'

'Joe,' said PK, 'I knew you'd hit the headlines one day.'

Nobody laughed at that though, so PK said: 'You're a slow lot today, aren't you?' So I did the face again. 'UHHH!'

'Right,' said PK, 'as I was saying before I was so rudely interrupted, what I want you to do is to empty out your mind. It's a bit like meditating – '

'What's meditating?' said Podge Grogan, who sits beside me, 'is that like deep-sea diving or somethin'?'

'Not quite,' said PK.

'Of course it's no!' says Lenny Poser Turnbull. 'Deep-sea diving!'

'Well,' said Podge Grogan, 'It coulda been! That's what it sounds like – deep-sea divin' in the Mediterranean Sea and that.'

'Aye!' I says, 'Deep-sea meditating – that's right, I've heard o that!'

'Away ye go!' says Lenny Turnbull, 'Deep-sea meditatin! Yez are off yer heids, you two!'

'Meditating,' says PK, 'as far as I know, has nothing to do with deep-sea diving at all, although, when you think about it, the two activities could be compared. You could say that meditating and deep-sea diving are . . . similar.'

So me an Podge Grogan turned round in our seats and looked at Lenny Turnbull.

'See?' says Podge, 'Deep-sea meditatin'. Tellt ye.'

'They're no the same at aw!' says Lenny Turnbull. 'Ah mean, ye dinnae need a harpoon tae meditate and that!'

'Ye dae in the Mediterranean!' says Podge.

'Aye,' I says, 'sharks and that. 'Course ye need a harpoon!'

'Aye,' says Lenny Turnbull, 'but you're talkin about deep-sea divin' – no meditation!'

'Well, Lenny', says PK, 'maybe you could tell the class what meditating is.'

'It's what they Buddhist monks dae.'

'Yes, but how do they do it?'

'They sit wi their legs crossed and chant an aw that.'

'Well . . . ' says PK, 'Yes, but – '

'Naw they dinnae,' says Podge Grogan, ''cause Ah've seen them. They dance aboot an shake wee bells tegither and sing Harry Krishner, that's how they dae it!'

'That's different,' says Larry Turnbull, 'that's no them meditatin', eh no, sir?'

'Well, no, I don't think so . . . in any case, there are different ways of meditating, but basically, what you have to do is to empty out your mind. You'll find that it's harder to do than you think. Your mind will keep thinking of things, all the little things we clutter our minds with every day – '

'How's that like deep-sea divin'?' says Lenny Turnbull.

'Well . . . it's hard to explain, Lenny,' says PK, 'I just meant that when you meditate you sort of dive into the depths of your mind. And that's what I want you to do. If you're lucky, you'll find something down there. Some treasure. A pearl.'

'Dae we get tae use harpoons?' says Podge Grogan.

'No, pens.'

'Awwww!' everybody says.

'Now listen,' says PK. 'It's quite simple really. All I want you to do is write in your jotter whatever floats into your mind. I don't want you to think about it too much, just let it flow. Okay?'

'OK, PK!'

'Anything at all. It doesn't have to be a story. It doesn't have to be a poem. It doesn't have to be anything. Just whatever comes into your heads when you've emptied your minds. Just let your mind *open up, open up* and let the words *flow* from your subconscious mind, through your pens into your jotters. It's called "automatic writing" and you're lucky to have a teacher like me who lets you do automatic writing, expecially first two periods on a Wednesday.'

This is still PK talkin', ken?

Then he says, 'I don't want you even to worry about punctuation or grammar or anything like that, just let your imagination roam free – not that you worry about punctuation anyway, you lot!'

So I says for a laugh, ken, 'What's punk-tuition, sir, is that like *learnin*' tae be a punk?'

Then everybody groaned.

'Joe,' says PK, 'will you just *shut up*.'

So I says for a laugh, ken, 'Hear that? First he's tellin' us tae *open up*, and now he's tellin' us to *shut up*!'

That got a brilliant laugh that.

Lenny Turnbull (poser) said, 'But sir, what if nothin' comes into yer heid when ye're sittin' there wi yer pen at the ready?'

'Anyway,' I says, 'how can I write anyway, 'cause I've no got a pen anyway?'

'Use yer harpoon!' says Lenny Turnbull.

'You can borrow this pen,' says PK, 'but it's more than this pen you'll need to write, Joe, because to write you also need inspiration.'

'What's that?' says Podge Grogan, 'a new flavour o chewing-gum?'

So I burst out laughin'. PK went spare again.

Then he brings this cassette out of his briefcase and says, 'Right, I want you to listen to this piece of music I've got here, so that it might give you some inspiration to get you going. Just listen to the music, empty your mind, and write down whatever comes out of the music into your heads. Okay?'

'OK, PK!'

'What is it, sir? Is it "The Clash"?'

'No,' says PK, 'It is none of that Clash trash. That Clash trash is even worse for your brain than video nasties *or* glue, Joe.'

Everybody laughed. So I did the face. 'UHHH.'

'If the wind changes, your face might stay that way,' says PK.

'Right, now stop wasting time. The music you're about to hear is not "The Clash" but a great piece of classical music by Johann Sebastian Bach.'

'Who's she?' says Podge Grogan.

'*He*,' says PK, 'was a musical genius who wrote *real* music, the likes of which you lot have probably never heard before and probably won't know how to appreciate even when you do. Now, I want you to be quiet and listen very carefully to this wonderful classical piece of music and just let go, *let go* and write absolutely anything the music makes you think and feel about. It is called, "Air on a G string".'

'Hair on a g-string?' I says.

Everybody fell about, ken?

'Come on now 4F, let's have a bit of order round here!'

Then Lenny Turnbull says, 'But sir, can we write *absolutely* anything we want, even swearin' and that?'

'Absolutely *anything* you want to,' says PK. 'Just listen to the music and *let go*. I promise no member of staff will see it, except me. If you don't want me to read it, I won't. The choice is yours. You can either read out what you've written to the class or you can give it to me and it will be destroyed. Okay?'

'OK, PK!'

Then Lenny Turnbull said, 'But sir, what about sex and that – can we put sex in it as well?'

'Hold on a minute,' says PK.

So I says for a laugh, ken, 'Hear that? First he's tellin' us to *let go*, and now he's tellin' us to *hold on*!'

That got a laugh, ken.

PK started clenching his fists, so the knuckles went all white, and he glared at me and his face went beetroot like he was going to go spare at me again.

'Look here, you lot,' says PK, 'we haven't got all day. You've wasted nearly a whole period already with your carry on and I am sick to the back teeth of having to RAISE MY VOICE IN HERE IN ORDER TO MAKE MYSELF *HEARD*! Will you please sit *still*, keep your hands on the *desk* and *you, Joe* Murdoch, are asking for *trouble*! One more wise crack out of you and you will be out that *door* and along to the *rector*, is that *clear*?'

'Yup.'

'As I was saying, you may write anything you like, but I don't think this piece of music will make you think about sex, because it is not an obscene bit of music at all. In fact, it is one of the most soothing pieces of music I know, so *shut up* and *listen*!'

So then PK gets the cassette machine out of the cupboard where it is kept locked up in case it walks, and he plugs it in and plays us this music. Everybody sits there and yawns.

Then Podge Grogan says, 'Sir, I've heard this afore!'

'Aye, so've I!' everybody starts saying. Then Lenny Turnbull says: 'Aye, it's that tune on the advert for they Hamlet cigars!'

So then everybody starts smoking their pens like cigars and PK switches off the music.

'Put your pens down!' says PK. 'Any more of this and I'm going to give you a punishment exercise and keep you in over the break! I am aware that this music has been used in an advertisement, but that is not the point of it at all. The point is, it was written centuries ago and it has survived even till today, so *belt up and listen to it*.'

So we all sat there and yawned till the music was finished, but nobody got any inspiration out of it to write anything at all.

So then PK says: 'If anybody is stuck, you could always write something or other about yourself. Describe yourself as others see you. 'Myself As Others See Me'. Now I've got a pile of prelims to mark, so I want you to keep quiet and get on with it.'

So here it is. This is my kreativ, automatic, deep-sea meditating writing:

MY OWN SELF AS OTHERS SEE ME

MY NAME IS JOE MURDOCH AND I AM SHEER MENTAL SO WATCH OUT. I HAVE GOT A GREEN MOHAWK. IT HAS GOT SCARLET SPIKES. ON MY FOREHEAD I HAVE GOT A SKULL AND CROSS-BONES. ON MY BLACK LEATHER JACKET I HAVE GOT 200 CHROME STUDS NOT COUNTING THE STUDS ON MY BELT AND MY DOG COLLAR. ON MY NECK I HAVE GOT A TATTOO IT SAYS CUT ALONG THE DOTTED LINE. ON MY BACK I HAVE GOT NO FUTURE. ON MY BOOTS I HAVE GOT NO HOPE. IN MY POCKET I HAVE GOT NO MONEY. MY MUM LOVES ME AND I LOVE HER BACK. MY DAD STOLE THE LEAD OFF THE DALKEITH EPISCOPALIAN CHURCH ROOF AND I GAVE HIM A HAND AND WE DIDN'T GET CAUGHT. I AM A WARRIOR AND I AM SHEER MENTAL SO WATCH OUT OK. THE END.

And now I will take it out to PK and tell him I don't want to read it out to the class, and I don't want him to read it either. I will tell him I want it to be *destroyed*. That should get a laugh, ken?

Exile

Robin Jenkins

About half-past twelve with a glass of sherry in her hand she went up on to the roof for, as she told herself, another stimulating look at the magnificent vista but really, as she knew, to watch out for the postman on his red motor-cycle.

Though it was mid-February the sun was warm and the sky blue. To the north soared the great pink lump of Montgo, reminding her a little of Suilven. To the east, bluer than the sky, stretched the Mediterranean all the way past the Balearics and Sardinia to Italy. Westward, beyond the groves of oranges and almonds, rose fold upon fold of hazy hills. Immediately below, to the south, lay the great plain of wild grass, small ploughed patches, and abandoned groves, frequented by flocks of small birds. Since this was Saturday she ought that afternoon to walk there calling on the birds to hide in holes or fly off to the hills, for tomorrow many Spaniards would come, after church, and shoot with alien zest every little living creature. She had come upon three murdered hedgehogs.

All round were blocks of flats gleaming in the sun. Like her own they were almost empty in winter. Except for the young Englishman and his Spanish girl friend she was alone in a building with twenty-six apartments. In every block, and most were much bigger than hers, were two or three British people, retired, come to live longer in the sunshine. In her wanderings whenever she met any of them she always found that, instead of having a great deal to say to them, as fellow castaways, no, as fellow adventurers, she had very little. They all seemed anxious, unsure, and even morose. A Tory all her life, she had nevertheless been shocked when the man next to her at the ghastly Christmas party at the restaurant *Casa Luis* had remarked that what Britain needed was a Franco to make the workers work harder and strike less.

All the time she was on the look-out for the postman. Suddenly her hand was shaking so much that she had to put down the glass. Her eyes filled with tears. Angry with herself, she twittered back at the house martins which came flitting over her head.

Unfortunately they reminded her of other birds in another place. In spite of her resolution not to let herself be seduced and tormented by nostalgic memories, she remembered the pigeons that used to fly down from the roofs to the playground after the children had gone in, and help themselves to the crusts, crisps, sticky papers, and 'douts' of apples left behind. She had stood in the doorway with the whistle in her hand and, though she had not known it at the time and therefore could not have shown it on her face, had loved those pigeons dearly.

Mr Proudfoot, the janitor, had apologized. 'I ken they're messy things. Miss Kilsyth was complaining the ither day aboot splashes on her windaes. But to tell you the truth, Miss Struthers, I like them. So do the weans.'

She had thought him a surly, discontented man, always grumbling about his union rights being infringed.

She remembered him too now with love.

A year or so ago, when she still got letters, she had been told in at least three that he had died suddenly of a stroke.

At last she heard and saw the postman. Yonder he was, a glitter of sunshine, speeding past the parador with its big palm trees, and past the beach deserted now except for some stray dogs. He stopped at the block of flats where the couple from Peterborough waited, often in vain, for a letter from their daughter in America or their son in Felixstowe. Soon he was on his way again, making brief stops at other blocks of flats, among them the one in which the woman from Yorkshire and her eight-year-old daughter were living. They had arrived only three weeks ago. Miss Struthers had met them in the supermarket. The woman had complained about the apartment she had rented: it faced the north and got no sun. The silent pale-faced child seemed to be no company for her.

The postman was chatting with the portero beside a big

bougainvillaea. They were in no hurry. They were at ease in their native sunshine. The many connections that anchored them so safely to their native place were unbroken.

Miss Struthers remembered the shops under those roofs where the pigeons had waited. Doig the butcher's. Jamieson the licensed grocer's. McKail the confectioner's. McAdam the baker's. Meikle the fruiterer's. And all the others, including the two public houses. She could picture in her mind the men and women who served in them. It was as if she had seen them just yesterday and not three years ago.

They had all said how lucky she was and how they envied her. Who with any sense would want to stay in dull, rainy, cold Scotland when there was the chance to live in sunny Spain? Those who knew her well, or rather those close to her, for nobody had known her all that well, had pointed out that the arthritis which had begun to make walking a bit painful would be cured or alleviated in the warmth.

Only one person had expressed misgivings. That was Mr Leitch, who had done odd jobs in her garden. In his brusque way he had said she was daft to go and bury herself among folk she didn't know, whose language three-year-olds could speak better than she. How was she going to pass the time, for God's sake? 'Well, for one thing, I could get to know Spaniards.' 'Not at your age, Miss Struthers. Nae disrespect meant. If onything I'm aulder than you. At oor age it's hard enough getting to ken folk that speak the same language as oorselves. Tak my advice. Bide here where you've spent maist o' your life and where you're kent.'

In spite of his pessimism he had wished her good luck.

As she watched the postman climb on to his motor-cycle again she wondered desperately who might have written to her. When she first came here she had had a letter almost every week. Colleagues, members of the Women's Business Club, neighbours, and acquaintances had written. She had eagerly and promptly answered every letter. As time had passed, though, her having exiled herself was no longer a novelty, letters had become scarcer and scarcer. Those that did come were brief and casual.

She had become aware that people whose lives had seemed dull and who indeed had often grumbled about that dullness were really so engrossed in their own affairs that it was easy for them to forget her.

Still, three weeks ago she had written to Margaret Lennox inviting her to spend her Easter holidays in Javea. Of all her colleagues she had liked Margaret best. In her invitation she had tried hard not to appear to be begging for an acceptance. Margaret too had never married. As the saying went, she had no ties. It would be easy for her to uproot herself for ten days.

Leaning over the parapet she watched the postman roar up the steep drive. She had learned to tell from the sound of the engine whether or not he was getting ready to stop.

She realized she was sobbing with anxiety.

'Don't be a wean, Jean Struthers,' she said sternly. 'If he goes by what of it? Some other day he'll stop.'

Yet, still silly as a wean, she was almost dizzy with hope and expectation when he stopped, climbed off, and took from his pannier bag an envelope. It was larger than the usual airmail letter, and it was brown, not blue. More than likely it was a circular for one of the absentee owners.

Without glancing up – why should it occur to him that he could be relieving a siege of loneliness that had lasted over six weeks? – the postman, whistling cheerfully, disappeared into the building.

Since there was no resident portero he had to put letters in the pigeon holes in the entrance hall. It had been peeping into Mr Williams' pigeon hole, and worse still by reading a postcard there, that Miss Struthers had discovered that his lady friend with the brown gypsy eyes and long earrings was known as Señorita Puig and not Mrs Williams.

The postman reappeared, climbed on his motor-cycle again, and shot off.

She did not rush downstairs. Drawing deep breaths, she forced herself to enjoy once again the sunlit view. Anyone who had known her would have thought that she was still the same Miss Struthers, calm, dignified, and self-possessed. They would never have guessed how her heart was racing, and how close to weeping she was.

Taking time to pick up the sherry glass and to drink what was left in it she went down to her flat. It was furnished in bright colours. The only piece of furniture that she had brought from home was an oak writing-desk that had belonged to her father. In it she kept all the letters she had received. They did not make a fat bundle.

She poured herself more sherry and slowly drank it, tapping with her fingers on the writing-desk. This was, she reflected, her third sherry of the morning. At lunch she would drink two, perhaps three, glasses of wine. In the evening, listening to the BBC or trying to for often reception was bad, she would have at least one brandy and water. She was drinking far too much. Her memories of home were most poignant when she was befuddled.

There was no lift, since there were only four storeys. Her flat was on the top. She went down the stairs not particularly slowly, for excessive slowness would itself have been a sign of impatience, but at a normal pace as if she was going to the supermarket. Her arthritic knee hurt, but she was used to that now.

Great joy, the big brown envelope was in her pigeon hole. But sometimes the postman in his hurry made mistakes. She had been disappointed more than once.

Wonder of wonders, the name on the envelope was hers. She did not recognize the handwriting but that did not matter. It was not as legible handwriting as it should have been but that did not matter either. The postmark was blurred but she thought it was her home town's. The envelope was quite bulky. Perhaps it was full of cuttings from the *Observer*, her home town's local newspaper. When she had been asked if she would like a copy sent to her every week she had, too curtly, refused. Where was the sense, she had thought, of beginning a new life hampered by intrusions from the old.

Up in her flat again, on the balcony that faced the Mediterranean, she slit open the envelope with a paper-knife made in Toledo. Inside was another envelope, and a letter so short that she almost whimpered with disappointment.

The address at the top was that of her school.

'Dear Miss Struthers,

I hope you'll excuse me writing to you. I'm a newcomer to the staff. The class I've been given was the one you had when you left. So they're eight-year-olds now. The other day they asked me if they could write a letter to you. So I said they could. Not all of them did. Some changed their minds and wanted to write to Dougal of the *Magic Roundabout* instead. I'm sure you'll understand. I thought you might like to see those that were written to you. I've not corrected the grammar or spelling. Some of what they say may look as if it has nothing to do with you, Miss Struthers, but I think that in everything young children do and say there is a lovely relevance.

Yours sincerely,

Alison Graham.'

Perhaps it was not Alison but Aileen. The writing hardly deserved four out of ten. The grammar too wasn't impeccable.

' "Lovely relevance", indeed!' murmured Miss Struthers, remembering many infantile stupidities. Then in a moment the phrase struck her as beautifully apposite. No doubt Miss Graham had untidy hair and skirts too short, but she certainly understood children.

Miss Struthers took out one of the letters. It was written on the page of a school jotter.

'Dear Miss Struthers,

I think you would like to no that I don't pick my nose any more you used to check me We have a new kitten called Snowy.

Jhon Garvie.'

She remembered him well, a nervous inattentive sandy-haired boy, son of a builder's labourer. God help her, she had made him sit with his hands behind his back.

She had not cherished him as much as she should.
She took out another. The writing was much neater.

'Dear Miss Struthers,
   My big sister was in Spain and saw a boolfight. There was
lots of blood. Oranges come from Spain. I hope your leg is
better. I think you are lucky to be in Spain for its raining today
and we wont get our game of rounders in the playground.
                                                    Mavis Hunter.'

She remembered Mavis too, very pert, plump cheeked,
always with a fresh ribbon in her black hair. Her father was the
town chamberlain. He wanted her to go to University one day.

There were at least twenty more. A gift of inexhaustible
riches. Reading them, and re-reading them, would make exile
no matter how long it lasted not only worth-while but also far
easier to thole.

The Star

Alasdair Gray

A star had fallen beyond the horizon, in Canada perhaps. (He had an aunt in Canada.) The second was nearer, just beyond the iron works, so he was not surprised when the third fell into the backyard. A flash of gold light lit the walls of the enclosing tenements and he heard a low musical chord. The light turned deep red and went out, and he knew that somewhere below a star was cooling in the night air. Turning from the window he saw that no one else had noticed. At the table his father, thoughtfully frowning, filled in a football coupon, his mother continued ironing under the pulley with its row of underwear. He said in a small voice, 'A'm gawn out.' His mother said, 'See you're no' long then.' He slipped through the lobby and on to the stairhead, banging the door after him.

The stairs were cold and coldly lit at each landing by a weak electric bulb. He hurried down three flights to the black silent yard and began hunting backward and forward, combing with his fingers the lank grass round the base of the clothes-pole. He found it in the midden on a decayed cabbage leaf. It was smooth and round, the size of a glass marble, and it shone with a light which made it seem to rest on a precious bit of green and yellow velvet. He picked it up. It was warm and filled his cupped palm with a ruby glow. He put it in his pocket and went back upstairs.

That night in bed he had a closer look. He slept with his brother who was not easily wakened. Wriggling carefully far down under the sheets, he opened his palm and gazed. The star shone white and blue, making the space around him like a cave in an iceberg. He brought it close to his eye. In its depth was the pattern of a snowflake, the grandest thing he had ever seen. He looked through the flake's crystal lattice into an ocean of glittering blue-black waves under a sky full of huge galaxies. He heard a remote lulling sound like the sound in a sea shell, and fell asleep with the star safely clenched in his hand.

He enjoyed it for nearly two weeks, gazing at it each night below the sheets, sometimes seeing the snowflake, sometimes a flower, jewel, moon or landscape. At first he kept it hidden during the day but soon took to carrying it about with him; the smooth rounded gentle warmth in his pocket gave comfort when he felt insulted or neglected.

At school one afternoon he decided to take a quick look. He was at the back of the classroom in a desk by himself. The teacher was among the boys at the front row and all heads were bowed over books. Quickly he brought out the star and looked. It contained an aloof eye with a cool green pupil which dimmed and trembled as if seen through water.

'What have you there, Cameron?'

He shuddered and shut his hand.

'Marbles are for the playground, not the classroom. You'd better give it to me.'

'I cannae, sir.'

'I don't tolerate disobedience, Cameron. Give me that thing.'

The boy saw the teacher's face above him, the mouth opening and shutting under a clipped moustache. Suddenly he knew what to do and put the star in his mouth and swallowed. As the warmth sank toward his heart he felt relaxed and at ease. The teacher's face moved into the distance. Teacher, classroom, world receded like a rocket into a warm, easy blackness leaving behind a trail of glorious stars, and he was one of them.

Tutti Frutti

Christopher Rush

Tutti Frutti, the boys called her.

It suited her, somehow: though once you thought about it for a moment it was clearly ridiculous and didn't apply to her in the least. She was totally without frills.

He vividly recalled the first time he ever saw her. She was kneeling down on the grass in her back garden, stroking Shakespeare, who had gone through the hole in the fence, exploring. He fell desperately in love with her at once. The time was out of joint: she was sixteen, he was fourteen. He was captivated, transfixed.

Naturally, he realized, he must have seen her without thinking about it, hundreds – no, thousands of times before. They had always been neighbours, his folks and hers, divided by nothing more than an old wooden paling.

And by religion.

They were Close Brethren, the Cargills.

That meant they would have nothing to do with the god of the Old Kirk, or the Congregational Kirk; or the noisy god of the Salvation Army, who marched down the pier, sounding brass and clad in scarlet and black. For that matter they had no truck with any of the other cells and sects in the salt-sprayed honeycomb of St Monans. They were on speaking terms with no god but their own. In Virgin Square Close Brethren meant what it said. Their god was a secret god, a god of whispers. You couldn't tell if he wore a cassock or a trench-coat. They went into their Meeting Place every Sunday and saw him privately, like the doctor. Then they came out and turned the key on him. Leaving him behind a blistered door and under a corrugated iron roof.

So when Sunday came Elizabeth disappeared for the whole day. That was the day she turned into a flower, pressed by the hushed pages of the big black book. Her sweetness was hidden away among sermons and texts, locked up in chapter and verse.

That at least was how he put it to himself, after a little fanciful consideration. He was learning to be a poet.

Somewhere between Genesis and Revelation lay his love.

Genesis: at a quarter to eleven every Sabbath the Cargill front door opened, and she – the beginning of all things – stepped out among the sparrows and seagulls. A parent on either arm. Her father was out of his yellow oilskins for Sunday and into black, the only colour suitable for this day of the week. Mrs Cargill wore black also. They were both grey-headed – douce, decent folk, quiet and gentle in their ways. Her mother was not one of those vultures that stood at corners and closes, stabbing at the remains of a reputation. Mr Cargill sailed with a religious crew, not with one of the drunken boats. She, their only child, had come to them late in life. A gift from God, certainly. Elizabeth.

Revelation: at twelve-thirty they came back along Shore Street, a sedate trinity, arm in arm. And if it was a warm day with a brightness on the waves, then she – the end of all things – would be wearing a white dress. He saw how closely they bound her to themselves, even to the front door; she, the white flower, pressed between the two black covers, the Lord's own script. The word of God. Elizabeth.

She was not allowed out on Sundays except to go to the Meeting. Sundays were strictly for church-going and bible-reading. During the week there was school, but she was in the fifth year at the Academy, and he was only in third. Their two orbits never intersected and she seldom appeared at nights. Saturdays were more hopeful. On Saturdays she helped her mother with the washing and the messages.

It was on a Saturday that he saw her – really saw her – for the first time, with the eyes of the poet-lover.

He saw Shakespeare go slinking under the paling. One of the boards had rotted at the bottom, leaving a spiky tunnel for him to pass freely from the one garden to the other. An irresistible means of feline ingress and egress. Following him, and hunkering down at the foot of the high fence, he found himself staring through a knot-hole at eye-level. He put his face close to the aperture – and there she was.

Stroking Shakespeare.

She was bent over the cat with her head on one side and one hand extended. Puss was primed for play and for adoration. He nosed her knuckles, cupped his paws around her waist and pretended to fall ineptly onto his back. Four legs and tail splayed absurdly wide, a furry starfish, so that his belly was vulnerable to tickles.

She tickled him. He squirmed. Clearly he was going to adopt her.

But it was the girl's face that mattered that morning. It was the first time in his life that he had actually studied a girl – and studied her without her having any awareness of it. She was ecstatic. Her lips were parted in a wide, almost pained smile. Her teeth were so white. She stroked the cat slowly, worshipfully, wordlessly. And he allowed her to manipulate him; he granted her the illusion of command. He was a living thing that she could caress as her own, not a fixed dogma, freezing her every gesture. She abandoned herself utterly to the cat.

She was not allowed pets.

That was how it happened: how he, who had never given girls a second thought, fell in love that Saturday morning. And to make the certainty absolute he went inside and confided it breathlessly to his diary. Yes, she was his Genesis and his Revelation, his alpha and omega; the first and the last. For fourteen years he had been living next door to a miracle of creation and he had never known it. His hand shook as he wrote.

> *Since first I saw your face I resolved*
> *To honour and renown you.*
> *If now I be disdained I wish*
> *My heart had never known you.*
>
> *What I that loved and you so liked*
> *Shall we begin to wrangle?*
> *No, no, no, my heart is fast*
> *And cannot disentangle.*

What was he to do? This business was entirely new to him. And no matter what he wrote or thought or said or did, she would never know how wildly he loved her and how fanatically devoted to her he was. Not even after he had courted and married her, she would never know.

But that was in the future. The immediate thing to do was to attract her attention and to please her at the same time. In both missions his dumb accomplice, willing or unwilling, he decided, would be Shakespeare.

No sooner do you conceive a revolution, he discovered, than something happens to frustrate and delay your bringing it off. The next day was Sunday, when she made her usual appearance: like a beautiful saying caught up between two black quotation marks, mysterious, untouchable, remote. The new minted image went down into the diary.

Monday began a week of the wickedest weather imaginable for May. Spring squalls in the morning shook the sea roughly and most of the boats bided their time. The sun appeared in bright bursts, but the winds worsened and rain hissed into the sun-streaked harbour so fiercely it seemed to be on fire.

He saw no sign of her at school. Mr Leslie launched himself tediously into Caesar.

> *For once upon a raw and gusty day,*
> *The troubled Tiber chafing with his shores.*

'Just such a day as this, wouldn't you agree, boy, or do you have troubles of your own? Whatever you are dreaming about, it certainly isn't Shakespeare!'

Of course, it was. Partly.

The sun went in for the rest of the week, crawling out stickily like a dismal slug. Every night after school he entrenched himself at the back window, hoping to glimpse her. The wind drove the raindrops grimly into the panes with sharp crackling sounds; he thought the glass would splinter. The back gardens glistened and streamed. Shakespeare sat by the fire like a cartoon cat and refused to acknowledge the back door.

Life was squalid. He closed his eyes and for hours on end he relived the scene of the previous Saturday: a girl stroking a cat, over and over, just behind his eyebrows.

'It's looking fairer,' his mother said to him, when Saturday came round again, 'and I haven't an egg in the house. Run down to Agnes Meldrum's and get me half a dozen.'

He was coming back past the west pier, clutching the eggs in a brown paper bag, when the loudest voice he had ever heard came clattering out over the harbour.

> *One o' clock two o' clock, three o' clock rock,*
> *Four o' clock five o' clock, six o'clock rock,*
> *Seven o' clock eight o' clock, nine o' clock rock,*
> *We're going to rock around the clock tonight . . .*

Provost Brand had opened his new café on Shore Street.

Having been kept in all week, many of the boats were ready to take the tide even though it was a Saturday. Some fishermen stopped what they were doing – battening hatches and stowing nets – to listen and stare. Most of them carried on with their chores, ignoring the alien racket. On the *Shepherd Lad* he could see Mr Cargill quietly coiling a rope, his grey head bent deeply into his work.

Fascinated, he drifted back to the café to look through the big plate-glass frontage. Frantic arms beckoned him. He went in. Some of his friends had put on long coats, drainpipe trousers and thick-soled shoes. They had slicked their hair, and one or two of them wore bootlaces for ties. The girls were in flared skirts with waspy belts; they were all polka dots and bobby socks and pony tails.

'Here, come and listen to this – it's great, man!'

He sat down at one of the tables. Everybody was drinking Coca Cola. All eyes were riveted on two constructions that squatted like buddhas against the far wall. One was a fat red refrigerator, a complex of chromium, levers and slots.

'Try it out, go on.'

He bought a Coke with the change from the eggs and placed his purchase in a cavity moulded to the bottle's fancy shape. A penny in a slot, a pull on a metal bar, and a cold Coke shot out from a chute at the other end, now a bronzed ingot of ice that burned his fingers.

The other god in the temple was the juke box. He had never seen such a monster. It was as big as a boat's wheelhouse. Behind the glitter and the glass were stacked all the latest musical hits. For a sixpence and the jab of a button a plastic arm swung out and brought in the selected record. The tables of teenagers listened in ecstasy. They looked at one another and grinned, and looked away in embarrassment.

Cigarette smoke misted the pounding air, a blue acrid haar; he shifted his seat to the window. Out in the harbour, and beyond that, in the firth, their fathers and grandfathers, their uncles and great-uncles, carried on the works and ways of the old days. In here the teenagers worshipped their new idols, thanked them that they no longer dressed and talked like *that* – not to mention listening to Jimmy Shand and "Abide With Me".

And sitting on the harbour wall, poised between the two traditions was – Tutti Frutti. A wave of panic went through him.

Yes, there she was, her message basket on her arm, talking to some of her classmates. They were all dolled up in their finery; the fifties had reached them right at the end of the decade. She had on a print frock and ankle socks and a navy blue donkey jacket; that was all. But she had her hair in a pony tail. Had it been like that last Saturday? He couldn't remember. It suited her, though, suited her large glasses and her open, honest face. Plain as she was beside all those birds of plumage, she was rarer than any of them.

Another wave hit him. Supposing she flew off and he never saw her again? Supposing he failed to capture her heart. Or what if one of the older boys came along right now and took her in hand? One of the boys in her year. Surely he couldn't be the only one in the universe to think her so beyond the epithets of beauty.

A knot of youngsters got up to leave and he sidled out with them over to the harbour wall, near to where she sat. Her friends were trying to tempt her inside.

'Oh, come on, Elizabeth, come in and listen. Just the one record.'

'I can listen out here. I'm not allowed.'

'Well have a Coke then. There's nothing wrong with a Coke, is there?'

'No, I can't, I can't. I'm not allowed.'

She wasn't allowed into Brand's new café. But that stood to reason. She was Close Brethren.

She wasn't allowed jewellery, make-up, scent; she didn't wear bangles or rings; she couldn't go to the Regal or the Empire in Anstruther, or to the pictures in Pittenweem; she wasn't permitted to go to the sixpenny hops or the dancing on the pier. There would be no radio in her house, no record player, and certainly no television set. The Close Brethren didn't even buy newspapers, and they gave house room to precious few books apart from the bible. Tutti Frutti wore no bobby socks, no bright scarves, no ribbons in her hair.

And she had no boy-friend.

Suddenly he felt a wash of gratitude towards her parents, those two black bookends. If it had not been for their strict ways she would by this time be inside Brand's café and would be the property of some lounger with a long jacket and greasy hair. She would be sitting on his knee and he would be holding her hand. No: this was the way it was meant to be. She had been saved – for him.

He stole a side glance at her. She waved once to that quiet grey man, her father. The *Shepherd Lad* was purring out of port. She left her friends and started for home. He followed her discreetly, locked to her in longing. In love.

Another Sunday. And nothing happened all day, except for that one bright sentence, briefly appearing between the black quotation marks, lingering poignantly in his memory like the smell of new-cut grass. Everywhere was so still. All the kirk bells boomed sadly, sullenly, at eleven o' clock, not just from the Old Kirk and the Cong, but from Elie and Pittenweem, even Anster three miles away. He could hear them all along the coast.

At school that week they'd been reading with Mr Leslie Charles Lamb's essay, 'The Superannuated Man'. He picked out one sentence from it –

Those eternal bells depress me

and entered it into his diary. He decided that from now on he was going to keep a Commonplace Book, like a real writer.

Halfway through another week, with dry weather, and still no sign of her. Then Mr Leslie said:

'I am trying – only trying, mind you – to lay the foundations for your Higher English, which you'll be sitting in two years time, like that cannon fodder down in the exam hall right now. Food for powder, I'm afraid, most of 'em, food for powder!'

So that was it. She'd be inside studying every night of the week. The Fifth Year were all taking their Highers. No wonder he'd seen nothing of her.

'Yes, that's right, boy, dream about it, dream about it, do. But you won't dream up a pass, I can tell you that, if you pay this little attention to your lessons.'

'Sorry, sir.'

'Yes. Dreaming of Glaramara's inmost caves. Or something.'

May slipped over into June.

The sea slid back over the weeded rocks, so far, it became little more than a blue lane running the length of the skyline, and the seaweeds popped and hissed and steamed. The sun simply forgot to leave the sky, the corn stood stalk still, breathless, expectant. At nights the Milky Way drooped its great branches low over the earth, dripping stars thickly onto the roofs. Out in the far firth the seals whooed and cooed like siren ghosts. His hands and face burned. Magic had returned to the old earth, myths were being spawned in the glitter of waves, faces appearing in the skellies and cliffs, new constellations flung up into space. Sleep was impossible by night, and concentration by day evaporated easily. Mr Leslie began to lose all patience.

'Write me a poem, dreamer. Write a whole cycle if you must. I am for whole volumes in folio, if necessary. But get it out of your system, whatever it is, and then get back to your English!'

He sat at the back window that evening and wrote in a hardback science notebook.

The sun whose beams most glorious are

Rejecteth no beholder.
And your sweet beauty past compare
Made my poor eyes the bolder.

Where beauty moves and wit delights
And signs of kindness bind me,
There, oh there, where'er I go,
I leave my heart behind me.

He was about to pen the next stanza when she stepped out of the back door. This was what he'd been waiting a lifetime for. He vaulted the banister and sped into the garden, snatching an astonished Shakespeare from the vestigial pleasures of a blue saucer. He bundled the cat, squirming, over to the fence, shoved it through its tunnel, and applied his eye to the knot-hole.

She was coming over to the fence already. Shakespeare was still standing there, his tail twitching, somewhat outraged at this unceremonious treatment meted out to a cat of his distinction. Closer she came, and closer. Dare he remain where he was? She might see his eye. But if he moved now she'd be more likely to spy a shadow. He held his breath and shut his eyes.

When he opened them again she was eighteen inches away, maybe less, he calculated. Nearer, nearer than he had ever been before. And so intent was she on the cat that she would have scarcely been aware of him even had the partition never existed. Though his heartbeats hurt and his head pounded, he was at liberty to make a cool study of her. She was his, just as the cat was hers. No-one had looked at her like this before. Yes, she was his, uniquely. He could see the china blue eyes, the flush of her complexion, pink over paleness, the two or three freckles on one cheek. Again her lips parted in that smile of abandonment, that ecstasy, as she stroked and stroked.

Shakespeare accepted this adoration as his due. He presented every curve and arch of his furred person to her reverential touch. Then, when she had catalogued his excellences from whiskers to tail, he leapt into her lap – she had on a sleeveless blue check pinafore – and stretched his front paws up onto her shoulders. She clasped him between her breasts and rocked him backwards and forwards in a smiling silence, her eyes tight shut.

The cat, with all the arbitrariness of his race, decided he'd had enough. He sprang over her shoulder, slashed at a stray galaxy of thistledown floating by, and streaked round the side of her house. Tutti Frutti lay on her back and communed with the sky.

That night as he lay awake he mentally charted her freckles. Were there three, or was there a fourth one just above the cheekbone? The question set him on edge with remembered excitement. He rose and put on his clothes.

It was strange to go padding about the house at this late hour of the night, when everyone else was asleep. Objects took on a curious new life of their own: his diary seemed to be listening and alive, his new Commonplace Book reading his thoughts; his various bindings looked out at him from their shelves, waiting to be read, sharing his secret. The conspiratorial thickness of the silence sent a shiver through his groin; he stood and tingled. He had never done this before, not in this way. Perhaps he was the only person in the village up at this hour.

Except for the fishermen, hauling somewhere out there on the watery world. He tiptoed to the back door and went out into the night, shivering through the dew-drenched grass, as far as the fence. He hauled himself up on one of the stobs and dropped down soundlessly on the other side. This was where she had been; she had occupied this very space that he was taking up. Right now he was inside her. At one.

A cold wetness on the back of his hand made him leap out of her skin. Shakespeare had followed him from the house. He sniffed and twitched for a minute. What was all this about?

Every house was darkened, every window containing a sleeper. The whole seatown was asleep. Strange, when you thought about it, that you couldn't actually hear anything of that combined rise and fall of many breaths. Maybe you could in one of the upland hamlets, with only cows and owls to break the heavy silences of fields and sky. But here everything was dominated by the huge hush of the sea, only yards away. Beyond the firth the ocean slurped slowly over the globe. Boats were working it even now, part of its cold poundings: his grandfather, his uncle.

Rocked on the bosom of the deep

Yes, they would be sweating at the nets, miles away, at the Dogger Bank or Peterhead. But only a few feet from where he stood, separated from him by a little night air, a few bricks and mortar, was the gently rising and falling bosom of Tutti Frutti.

Shakespeare had been rocked on that bosom. He had lain between her breasts. *Rocked on the bosom of the deep*. But then she'd had her dress on . . .

He looked up at her window. Vega burned like a torch over the fields.

Bright star, would I were steadfast as thou art –

He breathed the words quietly, religiously. Mr Leslie had begun Keats with them yesterday.

> *No – yet still steadfast, still unchangeable.*
> *Pillow'd upon my fair love's ripening breast,*
> *To feel for ever its soft fall and swell,*
> *Awake for ever in a sweet unrest,*
> *Still, still to hear her tender-taken breath,*
> *And so live ever – or else swoon to death.*

The sonnet was already down in his notebook. He longed to quote it to her. And so he would, he would –

> *Emprison her soft hand, and let her rave,*
> *And feed deep, deep upon her peerless eyes.*

But what if one night he should come out here and see her in her own bedroom, privately, the curtains undrawn, taking off her clothes?

Half-hidden, like a mermaid in seaweed

What if he should see the very parts of which Tutti Frutti was composed?

No.

Ravished by that thought, he swung himself back across the fence. Shakespeare hurried in at his feet, with dew-wet fur.

Once in bed he regretted his vision of a naked Tutti Frutti. She was a goddess. To hold her hand all day long would be enough. And at the end of the day, to remove her spectacles alone, and be granted a kiss.

On those chaste lips.

He spun himself into a wild web of dreams.

Next morning he slept late.

In the belfry of his head bells were booming, bells that sounded so far away. He was drifting past a foreign shore, out of reach of his own head. He stretched out his arm and woke.

He had been cast up on Sunday. And she would be at the Meeting. Shirt flapping over his jeans, he ran out, a disreputable wreck, onto the holy sands of the Sabbath. Overtaking the late stragglers, he arrived, panting, at the Meeting Place. He stopped outside its tarred bricks, sobered a little by the cold breezes that always blew round Virgin Square. A seagull sat on the funnel, listening to the holy din.

> *Wide, wide as the ocean,*
> *High as the heavens above,*
> *Deep, deep as the deepest sea*
> *Is my Saviour's love.*

Somewhere in the middle of that droning sea of voices was Tutti Frutti in her Sunday frock, singing palely between her mother and father. He stood and shivered outside her city walls throughout the length of the service. When the door finally opened he sprang away to a safe distance. Out she came, stepping stiffly between her bookends. He followed her home, a sly shadow in their religious wake. Saluting them as they passed the harbour were the strains of Buddy Holly from Brand's café.

> *Throughout the days*
> *Our true love ways*
> *Will bring us joys to share*
> *With those who really care . . .*

Once the Cargill door closed on her, he knew he would not see her again till the following week.

That Sunday was the longest he had ever known.

'It is midsummer's day today,' said Mr Leslie the next morning. 'Let us make shift to finish our *Midsummer Night's Dream.*'

> *The lunatic, the lover and the poet*
> *Are of imagination all compact.*

'Well, you'd have to be something of a lunatic, wouldn't you, to conduct a love affair through a wall?'

The Pyramus and Thisbe scene was duly completed.

'But it's as the poet said. Stone walls do not a prison make. Love has a way of overcoming obstacles. Read us the epilogue, boy.'

After school he tore a single sheet from an exercise jotter and wrote on it the three simple words, 'I love you'. He folded the page into a long strip, folded it again, then sought out Shakespeare. Tucking the missive tightly under the cat's collar, he waited by the back window. Soon after tea she came out. He took up the cat and carried it to the paling. As soon as it was through its tunnel he fled.

When Shakespeare returned he had nothing under his collar.

For the rest of that night he did not even dare go near the window. But when the house was asleep he rose up again from his bed and stole down to the harbour.

The tide was full, the sea calm, a few seine-netters lying quietly in their moorings; the harbour lamps, red and green, made trembling bridges across the water, from pier to pier; the boatyard was silent, the shops shut up. No old men at the corner, no conversationalists at the pier head; every house as tight and silent as a log. Only the stars and he were up and awake.

He shivered with the knowledge of it. And with the knowledge that only he understood the special holiness of this fishing village. Every slate, every stone, every boat and brick, every street she walked on, every wave that visited her shore – all were blessed by the fact that Tutti Frutti lived here. Asleep as she was, his consciousness of her overspread sea and earth.

And now she knew that somebody loved her – and she must surely know who that someone was. He had struck his blow. He took to his heels and raced madly along the sea front, Italian arias throbbing in his head.

The next day he sent her a Shakespeare sonnet, courtesy of Shakespeare.

> *Shall I compare thee to a summer's day?*
> *Thou art more lovely and more temperate.*

Puss returned with milk on his whiskers.
He sent her another.

> *O carve not with thy hours my love's fair brow*
> *Nor draw no lines there with thine antique pen.*

And another.

> *Being your slave, what should I do but tend*
> *Upon the hours and times of your desire?*

Shakespeare made the trips meekly and came back well contented. Sonnetless – but with the milk of paradise trembling on his wet whiskers.

He started to work his way through the sequence.

> *When in disgrace with Fortune and men's eyes . . .*

> *When to the sessions of sweet silent thought . . .*

> *When in the chronicle of wasted time . . .*

> *When I have seen by Time's fell hand defaced . . .*

Yet he could never bring himself to witness the moment of rapture. He fled from the knot-hole after each delivery. His mother began to tell him that he looked pale in the face.

'You're like a candle,' she said. 'Go and get yourself a fish supper!'

Shakespeare grew sleek.

'There are one hundred and fifty-four sonnets in the Shakespearean cycle,' said Mr Leslie at the start of the final week of session. 'No-one who has not read the whole of Shakespeare will ever be able to consider himself properly educated. Why not see to it over the summer? Vain hope!'

He calculated the number of trips Shakespeare would have to make. There were fifty-five days in the summer holidays.

But on the second last day of the term a policeman and a policewoman came to the Academy. And Tutti Frutti was driven away from the school.

In a police car.

Her friends stood in the playground, a white, shocked circle of faces. Their voices were hushed. Something had happened to Mr Cargill.

When he came home from the Academy at the end of the day, he found the Cargill curtains drawn. Out of respect, his mother had done the same, and so had some of the neighbours. The *Shepherd Lad* was on its way back from Peterhead. The word was all round the town.

After tea the west pier was crowded with folk, waiting. He could not bear to mix with them. He ran instead to the high kirkyard and stood at the dyke, looking out to sea.

He heard its engine before he saw the boat. It was a breathless evening, the sea laid out like a length of blue silk, only its hem rustling whitely.

Peering east, he saw the black speck off Pittenweem. Closer it buzzed, like an angry, ugly fly on the blue dress. Down on the pier the folk were pointing. Already they'd be saying it was the *Shepherd Lad* for sure, by the cut of its jib. It made a wide sweep, well past the May Island, before turning to starboard, as though unwilling to come into port.

It was a death ship.

Soon its engine was the only sound to be heard in the world, a harsh, dark drone, filling sea and sky. One or two gulls attended the death-boat. Bringing Mr Cargill home.

At the narrow harbour mouth the engine shut off and it glided through. The harbour accepted it quietly, like a soul to haven. Then the engine started up once more. The boat, a tormented heartbeat, churned its way to the west pier, hugging the old stones. He saw the mooring rope go snaking through the air to be caught by a hand somewhere in the crowd.

After that everything went quiet again. The awful cargo, tarpaulined, was brought out and transferred to the shore. Arms reached out. Hundreds of hands went up to heads and every cap came off. The village stood, the various sects, bareheaded under the one blue vault of the sky. They stood like that for one minute. Before the sound of many voices broke the stillness.

On his way home he passed groups of fishermen.

'No, it was his oilskins, caught in the winch. He was hauled in. You can picture the rest.'

'Picture it if you like. I'd forget about it if I were you.'

Forget about it.

How do you forget about it? A man had been pulled into the boat's winch and mangled. A grey-headed man of God. A bible-reading man.

He peered fearfully out of the back window. What was Tutti Frutti doing now in the dimness that lay behind these terrible curtains? They would be kept drawn now for three days, front and back. What was she thinking and feeling? Nothing of love, that was for sure. Nobody near and dear had died yet in his family, and he was fourteen. For years he had wondered what it would be like to be on the inside of one of these stricken houses, marked out by their shrouded windows.

The school broke up the next day. A generation of black and red blazers swarmed out of the building and broke up with shrieks and loud halloos. They were demented with joy. Everybody piled into Brand's café.

> *Got myself a cryin', walkin',*
> *Sleepin' talkin', living doll . . .*

Two days later the big black car hummed quietly up to the Cargill front door. The Close Brethren drifted in. There was no minister. Nobody knew in advance who would conduct the service, except that it would be some chosen person so moved by the Holy Spirit. One of their number would be saying the words right now.

> *Blessed are they that mourn: for they shall be comforted.*

> *The souls of the righteous are in the hands of God, and there shall no torment touch them. They are in peace.*

The door opened and out came the box, borne on a black wave that drowned the sun. And the black snake of mourners gathered, arranged itself, shuffled its feet, and moved off, drawn by that gleaming black head, the hearse. A head crowned with flowers. Neither Tutti Frutti nor her mother were there. Women did not go to funerals. The last they ever saw of their menfolk was when they were carried out of the door.

But at every corner stood knots of men. When the hearse passed them they put their hats and bonnets to their chests and bowed their bare heads, like actors at the end of a melodrama. Then they joined the cortege at the tail end. So, at every turning point, the snake increased its length, grew more tramping feet. The sound of polished boots crackled against the wash of the water. Brand had shut off the juke box for the afternoon.

He raced over the barley field to reach the kirkyard by the back way, well before the mourners. The inevitable gull stood sentinel on the kirk steeple, a gleaming white sea-angel. It watched the black snake toiling up the kirkyard hill and breaking into pieces at the graveside. The snake's head opened and its mystery was removed: the polished box with the dark shine and the coldly glittering name place. Mr Cargill was lowered into his fathom of earth, underneath the turf.

Silence.

And like a cracked bell came the words – familiar, dreary, comforting as the tides.

> *I am the Resurrection and the Life, saith the Lord: he that believeth in Me, though he were dead, yet shall he live: and whosoever liveth and believeth in Me shall never die.*

The words were heavy as clay, but they glinted like newly turned clods after the rain.

> *I heard a voice from heaven saying unto me,*
> *Blessed are the dead which die in the Lord*
> *from henceforth: yea, saith the Spirit, that*
> *they may rest from their labours; and their works*
> *do follow them.*

A voice inside him sneered, But they don't rest from their labours, they just die and are forgotten.

'No!' he shouted out loud. 'That's not true!'

Some of the mourners raised their heads in his direction. He ducked down behind the dyke.

A new breeze rustled the barley.

The gull left the steeple then and winged its way east. Out in the bright firth the fishermen carried on with their labours. Except for the crew of the *Shepherd Lad*. And a cloud of white birds followed them.

He went back home through the barley, and he sat down and wrote in his Commonplace Book.

> *Only Love and Death change all things.*

The barley turned with the season.

Tutti Frutti did not return for her Sixth Year. She left school and went up to the Art College in Dundee.

The barley-wave was yellowed, stubbled, darkened by the plough, whitened by winter, pricked by spring, greened over again by summer.

A boy from his class took a berth on the *Sherpherd Lad* following the death of another of its crew. He was not a Brethren worshipper; he worshipped in Brand's café every Sunday. But his folks at least were members of the Old Kirk. And the boat needed a cook.

'You are all in it up to your necks,' snapped Mr Leslie. 'The Highers will not go away like a bad dream. And time marches on!'

He sat at his table by the back window night after night,

bent over his books. Down in the garden Shakespeare lazed about without a care in his belly. The little tunnel to Tutti Frutti's house was overgrown by now, and in any case he preferred the opposite garden these days. There was a fluffy creature called Samantha on that side.

By the time he sat his Higher English Samantha had had kittens.

Twice.

'You could do a degree in English,' Mr Leslie said to him at the start of his last session. 'You have a fine feeling for literature.'

The field-wave undulated once more under the wind of the seasons.

St Andrews University accepted him for an Honours course in Mr Leslie's subject.

He was lying reading in the hot grasses of August, waiting for the long summer to pass, when he saw her for the last time. She was wearing a mini-skirt and a cutaway blouse that left her brown midriff bare. The pony tail was still with her, and the glasses. She was walking west the braes towards the kirkyard, hand in hand with her boy-friend. He was one of the Jesus boys – all beads and beard and sandals and hair. They had a transistor with them that was playing fuzzily.

She'll switch it off, surely, he thought, when they go into the kirkyard.

But they didn't go into the kirkyard, where Mr Cargill lay. They walked right past, and as they reached the crest of the hill, the transistor cleared.

A smash hit single, announced the strident voice of the disc jockey – by an exciting new group called The Beatles.

> *Love, love me do,*
> *You know I love you,*
> *I'll always be true,*
> *So ple-e-e-ease*
> *Love me do.*

The sounds died away as the twisting, laughing couple disappeared over the shoulder of the hill, holding hands. He stared down into his well thumbed copy of The Works of Shakespeare. Then he shut the fluttering pages, got up stiffly, and walked away.

Outside Brand's café he stopped. The same single was playing in there. He went inside, bought a coffee, put money into the juke box, and sat down with his book.

His song came on.

> *You go your way and I'll go mine,*
> *Now and forever till the end of time,*
> *I'll find somebody new, and baby,*
> *We'll say we're through,*
> *And you won't matter any more . . .*

'Buddy Holly!' the girl in the corner muttered to her friend. 'Can you credit it?'

Her lip lifted.

He put his chin on his book and stared out to sea.

The two of them looked at him in disgust.

The Tree and the Harp

George Mackay Brown

So, the dreadful old woman was dead at last. Old rich Mrs Maida was lying still and cold in her bed in the big house called the Hall.

The Hall stood down at the shore, an eighteenth-century house with a large garden surrounded by a high wall, so that Mrs Maida might have privacy from the coarse islanders.

One or two islanders there had to be inside the precincts, the two gardeners, (one of whom, Sam; looked after the hives and the honey) and Miss Troll, the housekeeper who lived in the lodge, – she had learned her trade in rich important houses in the south, and was even snootier than old Mrs Maida, though more prim – and Mrs Birsay the cook and cleaner, and Mrs Birsay's girl Sophie, aged twelve. (Mrs Birsay was a widow.)

Sophie was glad that Mrs Maida was dead. She didn't exactly sing and dance; but she felt a shadow lift from her. That terrible voice, that sarcasm that was like the flash and bite of a sword, would frighten Sophie no more!

At breakfast-time her mother had come downstairs and whispered in the kitchen, 'She's dead! Poor Mrs Maida died in the night . . . ' And then touched her eyes with the corner of her apron; for Mrs Birsay was a gentle-hearted woman. She had suffered greatly under Mrs Maida – no tyrant could have afflicted a loyal subject so horribly.

And Sophie wept to see her mother weeping. But inside, her heart was like a bird.

Only two weeks since that black voice had been ringing through the big house. 'Woman, this steak pie isn't fit to eat!' . . . 'You, woman, what d'you call yourself, Mrs Birsay, I nearly broke my teeth on the buns you baked this morning'

. . . 'Birsay, you slut, there's a cobweb on the painting of my grandfather the general – there, woman, at the corner of the frame – clean it at once!' . . . 'No, I do *not* want a cup of tea. Say tea to me once more and I'll strangle you.'

And Sophie's mother had taken all these lies and insults and said nothing.

She knew her place, Sophie's mother.

Besides, if Mrs Maida had dismissed her, which she might well have done in one of her terrible tantrums, where could mother and daughter have gone?

There was no place in the world for them. Nowhere.

Sophie's father had been a sailor. They had lived in a rented house in the village. One winter, when Sophie was ten, a telegram had come – Bill Birsay had been lost at sea, swept overboard in a gale in Biscay.

They had had to be out of the house by November. After the grief, that was a gnawing worry. They had no relatives in the island. They were alone, and poor.

For many nights that summer Mrs Birsay and Sophie sat silent, looking into the fire, the tea growing cold in their cups.

Occasionally a man with a brief-case from the National Assistance office would come and ask tart questions.

One night there had come a prim knock on the cottage door. It was prim Miss Troll from the big house. 'It has come to Mrs Maida's notice that you might be available for general duties up at the Hall. Cooking and cleaning. Mrs Maida is very particular. She has a delicate stomach. She cannot bear untidiness in any shape or form. Please come to be interviewed at the Hall by Mrs Maida tomorrow morning at 10 am. Should you prove acceptable, a room will be provided for you and the girl.'

And Mrs Birsay had gone to be interviewed – a harrowing experience – and she had been accepted. She was to start on Monday morning. Ten pounds a week, room and fire and food free; Wednesday afternoons off.

Mrs Birsay could have hugged Mrs Maida with gratitude.

But one look from that basilisk eye quelled her.

'Thank you, ma'am,' murmured Mrs Birsay, and curtsied.

And so mother and daughter moved into the big house, at the beginning of spring.

And really, it was a nice little room on the ground floor they had, with a rosebush outside the window, and blackbirds singing from morning to night, and pigeons hopping and cooing round the kitchen door.

The garden was lovely. A little burn crept through it and out into the sea beyond the high wall. The burn, unfortunately, was sluggish and weed-choked and muted. Under the single tree it broadened into a dark deep pool, that looked sinister in the sunlight.

It would have been heaven for Sophie, if it hadn't been for the tyrant on the floor above. 'Listen, Mrs Birsay or whatever you call yourself, I can't eat soup with carrots or peas or onions in it. Please remember that!' . . . 'Woman, I didn't sleep a wink last night – you made the bed up all wrong' . . . 'Mrs Birsay, I don't want that girl of yours – what's her name, Sophie – wandering all over the garden. She'll ruin the flower-beds. *There's to be no climbing up that sycamore tree beside the pool* – I will *not* have your girl doing that' . . . 'Woman, come here at once – drop everything, a button has come off my blouse, sew it on' . . . 'How many times do I have to tell you, I only drink tea with my breakfast' . . . 'Do you ever think of anything but tea?' . . .

So began this hideous tyranny that lasted for six months.

It had to be put up with. There was nothing else for it. Apart from the ten pounds a week, they were slaves.

How Sophie would have loved to wander through the forbidden garden! But if she set foot beyond the pavement that girdled the house one or other of the gardeners was there to shoo her away. They had been given their orders.

Even after the gardeners went home, at sunset, it was impossible. Mrs Maida was always on the watch from her high window, like a hawk.

But one night of full moon Sophie did it! Her mother was

busy in the kitchen, preparing tomorrow's dinner. Miss Troll had gone to a church meeting. The tyrant had been in bed all day with a headache; her curtains were drawn.

Sophie looked; the curtains were still drawn. The moon had risen clear of the high garden wall. Beads of dew flashed from the flower-beds near and far, in the light of the full moon. And now the moon was looking through the sycamore leaves into the pool.

It was pure enchantment.

It was more than Sophie could bear.

She went like a shadow across the lawn. She stood under the tree. She seized the lowest branch and swung herself up into the tree. And the leaves whispered all about her.

Sophie looked down into the pool. It was dark and stagnant and sinister.

Then she heard a voice. 'Hello, I wish I had known you. Thirty years ago – thirty Julys – I sat in that tree. You're the first girl to sit in that fork of the tree since that night thirty years ago. Welcome.'

Sophie was so startled she almost fell out of the tree. The voice had been sweet, distinct, beautiful.

Yet it was difficult to locate the music of the voice, precisely. There was certainly no one to be seen, neither in the tree nor at the pool's edge nor among the bushes and flower-beds.

Sophie was on the point of dismissing the words as a part of the night's enchantment (for everything was lovely beyond words, really, and made perilous by the deep dark flashing pool below, and by the possibility that a dreadful eye was looking at her from the edge of a curtain). Oh, she had never felt so moved and excited! She would tell nobody, not even her mother.

Now she *must* go in. She would be missed.

'I was a girl once, too.'

There was no mistaking the voice this time.

There was sadness in it, and loss, and pleading.

57

Sophie looked everywhere.

There was no girl to be seen.

Then the moon went behind a cloud.

Sophie dropped out of the tree. She moved across the garden like a shadow.

'Where have you been, Sophie? You look as if you'd seen a ghost. I'll put on the kettle for tea. Have you done your lessons? Oh, dear, I hope Mrs Maida will like this roast chicken, cold! I know it'll be good' . . .

Mrs Maida did not like the roast chicken. For five days she liked nothing that was offered to her.

She lay in bed, sipping barley water, with the blinds drawn, growling and complaining.

'Something, woman – surely there's *something* you can cook that'll lie on my stomach . . . That custard was like yellow peril – take it away . . . Can't you even poach an egg properly? – I've had heartburn all day after that egg' . . . No, I do *not* want a nice cup of tea! . . . '

If it wasn't the food, it was something else. 'This pillow's as hard as a stone' . . . 'I said I wanted a hot-water bottle, not a wishy-washy lukewarm thing' . . . 'That girl of yours, Sophie, makes far too much noise in the morning going to school – clack clack clack over the paving – can't you get her a pair of soft shoes?' . . .

No doubt about it, the tyranny in the big house was growing blacker and heavier.

Even Miss Troll felt the lash of that tongue, and would pass up and down stairs with thin grey lips.

As for Mrs Birsay, nothing she did was right.

Sophie knew that her mother was the very best cook and housekeeper in the island.

It was shameful, the way she was treated.

One had to make allowances for an invalid. But it was very difficult.

Now old Mrs Maida was more often in bed than out of it.

Dr MacIntyre called every day. Not even he was spared.

'Are you sure you're a proper doctor and not a quack? That last bottle you gave me nearly killed me. I want another prescription this time – something quite different. I sometimes think I'd be better with a tinker wife and her herbs' . . .

If, once or twice, Sophie came face to face with the dreadful old woman in the long corridor, she turned and fled! 'That's right, you little brat, off with you, get your mother to poison you with that awful tea she's forever making' . . .

But those chance encounters became fewer and fewer.

The old tyrant was getting weaker, no doubt about it.

Now, in late summer, she only got out of bed to shuffle on Miss Troll's arm to the garden chair between the rose bush and the fuchsia bush.

'Not there, you fool!' she wheezed one day when Miss Troll had set the garden chair for her under the sycamore tree, beside the pool. 'You ought to know better! Over there, beside the red roses . . . '

But, after five or ten minutes, it was, 'The bees are bothering me . . . There, I've got hayfever again – it's that farmer cutting his hay. I could wring the fool's neck . . . Take me inside.'

Illness had made her more dreadful, in Sophie's eyes. She glared here and there out of her grey shrunken mask of a face.

And Miss Troll had to summon Mrs Birsay to help carry the old rich wreck of a woman up to her bed.

Only twice in the month of August did Mrs Maida venture into the beautiful garden – and then only briefly. The butterflies revelled silently about her departure, as she hobbled in on Miss Troll's arm.

And the two gardeners would light their pipes and have a rest. It was a large house of twenty rooms. For Sophie, it was forbidden territory; she was confined to the bed-sitting room and the kitchen.

'Oh,' her mother would cry, 'It's such a sad house! All the

rooms blinded, all the lovely furniture covered in sheets. The loveliest room of all is the music room. Oh Sophie, how I wish I could take you to the music room! But I can't. Mrs Maida has forbidden it, strictly.'

(Mrs Birsay had to dust the deserted part of the house twice a week.)

Sophie's curiosity, as harvest-time came and the farm-folk cut their barley in the fields around, narrowed to the music room. Sophie loved music, but – other than sing – she had no chance to do anything about it. To play the piano well was her greatest ambition. But that was out of the question; there was no piano available, and furthermore her mother couldn't afford to send her to the lady in the village who gave piano tuition.

As the darker nights of autumn drew in, Mrs Birsay spent most of her time sewing and knitting. Now the mistress of the big house could take only the lightest of food; fruit juices, poached fish, beaten-up eggs. So Mrs Birsay justified her existence by knitting bed socks for the invalid, and making curtains of the old rich materials she had found in a chest in the attic; so that it might cheer up the invalid.

But all she did was grumble. Nothing was right. Her voice had lost its black edge. It was old and grey and hopeless now.

'What do I want fine curtains for? They should have been hung thirty years ago . . . What did you say the name of your girl was? Sophie? Tell Sophie she can sing if she wants to – she has a nice voice. I heard her the other evening, singing under my window . . . No tea, not even for breakfast – it tastes of nothing . . . Nothing tastes of anything any more . . . I feel very tired . . . Tell that Troll woman not to come near me. She looks more and more like an undertaker or a gravedigger . . . The curtains are quite pretty, Mrs Birsay, but they're thirty years too late . . . Tell Sophie she is *not to go into the garden* . . . '

It was pathetic, Mrs Birsay told Sophie, to see how weak and shrunken the old lady had become.

'I think,' said Mrs Birsay, 'she'll never be out of that bed again . . . '

Why did those words put a sudden glitter in Sophie's eyes?

The big house was quiet after tea.

Miss Troll had gone to visit another spinster who lived at the far end of the island, on WRI business.

Mrs Birsay was sewing cushion covers out of the roll of material she had uncovered in the attic. The mistress had said she could do anything she liked with it. Mrs Maida, once her health began to improve, might enjoy bright cushions in the rooms, instead of the old sun-faded ones. So Mrs Birsay sewed and hemmed and drank endless cups of tea.

The old invalid was presumably drowsing in her bed. More and more she was lost under the tides of sleep.

Sophie, without a word, slipped out of the room, and began to explore the house. She carried a candle with a yellow flower of flame floating above.

Where was the music room?

Oh, it was eerie! Sophie opened room after room – each, in the candle-light, was an immense silent theatre of shadows. The shadows crowded about her. All the chairs and tables covered, as if they were dead and waiting for the worms. Sophie shut door after door. Her thudding heart must be the loudest thing in the house.

Once a drop of hot candle wax fell on her hand! She almost screamed.

She opened a door. Another dance of shadows, a silent gathering. Ah, but this must be the music room. That shrouded shape over there could only be the piano! Sophie moved over towards the piano. Her glimmer of light discovered a white bust on the mantelshelf, with the name 'Chopin' on the base – and over there, against the wall, a Celtic harp. Sophie touched a string – it gave out a rich pure note – the whole house seemed to echo the golden sound.

A voice said, 'Oh, if I had known you thirty years ago! . . . We would have had such happy times . . . Yes, I'd have taught you to play the harp, and the piano too . . . I think I'd have had no better friend than you . . . Too late, too late . . . '

The voice was clear and unmistakable; it was the voice she had heard in the garden.

This time, there was no enchantment of moonlight to shake it out of the nothingness; only a feeble candle-flame, and a harp stroke.

Sophie was not in the least afraid: there was such an air of welcome in the music room, though it was tinged by sadness and regret, a little.

The reverberations of the harp stroke seemed to go on for a long time. Then the room was stark and cold again.

Sophie stayed there as long as she dared.

She *must* go back – she would be missed. (She ought to have been bent over her home-work.)

She descended the wide stair, softly, led by the yellow petal of flame.

Coming round the corner into the long corridor that ended in the kitchen, Sophie almost ran into a frail figure lingering at the foot of the great stairway.

The girl cried out with terror! It was Mrs Maida. The candle fell on the floor and went out.

The old woman put leaf-light hands on Sophie's shoulder. 'Sunniva, I heard you at the harp, dear,' she said. 'It was lovely. I thought there would never be music in this house, ever again . . . Oh, I know it's lonely for you here in this big house, I know it is. I can't think what to do about that, Sunniva. You can't mix with the village girls. That's out of the question. I know you'd like to speak to them, maybe invite a girl or two up to the house. I'll think about it. Maybe some day. It's hard to know what to do for the best . . . If only your parents were still alive . . . Yes, dear, you can walk in the garden if you like. It's such a lovely night. Then supper and bed. What, you'd like to climb up into that tree? I don't see why not. You're light and strong enough . . . '

What was the old woman talking about?

'I'm Sophie,' said the girl. 'I'm sorry for wandering about the house like this. I didn't do any harm.'

'Come and kiss me goodnight once you're in from the garden, Sunniva,' said Mrs Maida in a gentle voice.

Then she put her twisted hand on the banister and began slowly to climb the stair to her room.

That night, she died.

Miss Troll came into her own, briefly, making arrangements for the funeral. Only the gentry were invited, of course, and the village merchant and the farmer from the big farm and the local councillor and Dr MacIntyre. As things turned out, very few attended the funeral in the little family burial-place next to the Hall. The weather was bad. And nobody had liked the dead woman very much.

Miss Troll had done the things that ought to be done at a funeral. There was sherry for the mourners, and plates of smoked salmon on toast, and little cakes that Mrs Birsay had made. The few mourners lingered awhile in the drawing room, made a few valedictory remarks, then went away with their long insincere faces.

Miss Troll permitted herself a thin smile as the last of them went. She had done her duty.

Neither Mrs Birsay nor Sophie had been invited to the funeral, of course.

Mrs Birsay had the longest face of all, not only that day but for several days to come. From time to time she touched her eyes with the corner of her apron. The kettle was always on the boil. The teapot was never empty.

What would become of her and Sophie now? Once more they would be out in the cold winds . . .

'You may stay where you are meantime,' said Miss Troll. 'Mrs Maida was the last of the family. No doubt the house will be sold. The family lawyers in Edinburgh have the disposing of the estate. We will just carry on as we're doing until we receive official notice . . . No doubt my services to Mrs Maida, extending over forty years, will not be forgotten' . . .

This last sentence was spoken with a tinge of anxiety. It was obvious that Miss Troll was not at all sure as to how things would fall out. If she had been, she would not have spoken the way she did to a mere servant like Mrs Birsay. It was the first time Miss Troll had ever visited the Birsays' room.

As the days passed, anxiety began to eat into her more and more. She took to visiting Mrs Birsay twice or thrice a day in the kitchen. (Mrs Birsay was a good listener.) She even condescended to drink cups of tea.

'I was very faithful to Mrs Maida,' she said; permitting Sophie's mother to pour her yet another cup of tea. 'I might go so far as to say, I sacrificed my prospects for her. For, after the terrible thing happened, she was almost out of her mind. Had I not been there to support her who knows what she might not have done? I was a rock of strength to her, when she needed me most. And I devoted all the rest of my days to her. I'm sure she won't have forgotten me in her will. But did she ever *make* a will? She didn't like talk of death and wills and tombstones – she couldn't stand the thought of her latter end. The lawyers in Edinburgh, they must know what I've sacrificed for Mrs Maida' . . .

So that was it – the prim proud spinster was even more terrified than Mrs Birsay as to what might become of her, now that the earth had closed over the mistress of the house.

She had lived for forty years in the lodge at the end of the drive: it was a part of her; it was unthinkable that ever she might have to leave it.

'There are no immediate relatives,' said Miss Troll. 'There are, I think, some distant cousins in Canada and South Africa. They were little help to her when the tragedy happened. They never even wrote a letter of sympathy. In fact, I doubt if Mrs Maida had even *seen* them all her life long. How awful, if they were to inherit the estate!'

'Well,' said Mrs Birsay, 'it must have been a sad thing for her indeed, losing her husband.'

'Pooh!' said Miss Troll. 'She never shed a tear for *him*. Mr Maida had his own house, in Perthshire. I quite liked Mr Maida, he was always civil to me. Then suddenly he left, without so much as a goodbye. Mind you, Mrs Maida could sometimes be a difficult person to live with. Between you and me, but for

Charles, their son, he'd have left her much sooner. As soon as Charles was found a suitable position in the city, and settled, Mr Maida was up and off' . . .

'A son!' cried Mrs Birsay. 'So there's a son!'

'There *was* a son,' said Miss Troll. 'He was killed in a car crash in Yorkshire, himself and his wife, two years after they were married. They were on their way north, for a holiday, with the baby, to see her.'

'That was a terrible thing to happen!' said Mrs Birsay. 'No wonder she had her dark moods from time to time.'

'She didn't roll a tear down her cheek for that either,' said Miss Troll. 'Not one single tear, that ever I saw. She was like one of those ancient Roman matrons you read about – all strength and resolution.'

'And the baby, it was killed too?' sighed Mrs Birsay.

'Oh, no. The child survived . . . "What home or institution will I place the creature in?" Mrs Maida said twenty times if she said it once in the course of the next few days, while the funeral arrangements were going on. (Mr and Mrs Charles are buried out there too, in the same place as the mistress.) "I can't have a brat about here," she declared. "I couldn't put up with it for an hour" . . . Then suddenly, on the evening of the double funeral, she rounded on me and she declared, "Troll, I think I'd better have this grandchild here. I'll give it a try, anyway" . . . '

'The poor child!' said Mrs Birsay – and at once she could have bit out her tongue for saying it.

'Not poor child in the slightest,' said Miss Troll. 'I never in my life beheld such a beautiful happy child, right from the start. And that same child caused a miracle in this house. The stream ran, the desert blossomed as a rose. That same child, I assure you, gave Mrs Maida twelve years of the most wonderful happiness! It was a blessing in her life. This house seemed to be overflowing with music and laughter all the time . . . Ah, she played the piano like an angel, Sunniva. Alas!'

'What happened?' whispered Mrs Birsay, and brought the corner of her apron up to her eyes again.

'You see that tree out there in the garden?' said Miss Troll.

'Over there by the pool. One summer evening Sunniva – that was her name – climbed up into the tree. A branch broke. She fell into the pool and was drowned. Nobody saw it. The gardeners lifted her body out of the pool next morning, and carried it into the house. "Lay her in the music room," said Mrs Maida coldly . . . '

Mrs Birsay choked on her sobs; beyond speech she was.

'From that day,' said Miss Troll, 'winter and night descended on this house. I thought, for a month and more afterwards, that she would go mad. Dr MacIntyre shook his head. "It's more than you or I can handle, Miss Troll," he said. "If she could weep," he said "she might improve. As things are, she'll will herself into the grave. What's the name of that old Greek sculptor whose statues seemed to have the breath of life in them? – here we have the opposite process, a living woman turning herself to stone in front of our eyes. I can't do a thing about it" . . . For a month she did not speak. She hardly moved. I think, though, she cried in secret. I would see her, morning after morning, with the stains on her face. Then one morning she spoke. "Troll," she said, "I want all the rooms closed up. Cover the furniture. Draw the blinds. Stop the clocks. Only the needful rooms are to be used" . . . So, in a way, she recovered. But the terrible scar was in her mind and heart and spirit to her dying day . . . Not that she ever mentioned Sunniva. One day, some time later, I happened to say, "That sycamore, it might be better cut down, don't you think? And the pool is stagnant – it ought to be drained?" . . . Oh, Mrs Birsay, I have never before or since endured such a storm of rage! The tree and the pool would stand till they rotted! I was never to mention such a thing again . . . Poor silly me, I never know when enough is enough – I suppose it might have been a year later that I said, "Mrs Maida, the girl Seenie", (Seenie used to come twice a week to dust and polish) – "Seenie," I said, "tells me one of the harp-strings is broken in the music room. Will I have it seen to?" Such a sudden blaze of anger! "Nobody is to touch a thing in the music room, now or at any other time. Never so much as mention music room again, you withered old witch!" . . . So, Mrs Birsay, I learned my lesson the hard way. Many a time I was sore tempted to leave her. But time passed, and I grew older, and at last I knew I would stay with her till the end.'

'I have never heard anything so sad!' sighed Mrs Birsay. 'Poor Mrs Maida – I forgive her the one or two hard things she said to me.'

'It's come at last,' said Miss Troll, producing a letter from her handbag. 'A solicitor from the firm in Edinburgh is coming on Monday. For some reason, he wants to see you and Sophie also. I suppose it's a good sign that the letter's addressed to me . . . No, thank you, Mrs Birsay, I won't have any more tea.'

Miss Troll's hand trembled as she put the letter back into her handbag.

Sophie raced through the big house, room after room, pulling up blinds, tearing the covers from chairs, tables, sideboards, throwing open the windows so that, after thirty years' stagnation, the air could flow in.

She was behaving like a crazy girl.

Sometimes she laughed. Sometimes she cried. She had to sit down, from time to time, for a little rest. But never for long. It was out into the corridor with her, into another room: the blinds jerked up, window sash opened, covers whisked off. Beautiful hidden objects declared themselves: clocks, bookcases, bowls and jars of great beauty, tapestried chairs, portraits in gilt frames, round oak tables.

And they were all hers!

Sophie threw open a high drawing-room window. The two gardeners, Sam and Willie, were idling below – since Mrs Maida's death they had turned noticeably lazier. 'Hey, you two!' shouted Sophie. 'I want that pool under the tree cleaned out at once. Do you hear me? I want the burn to go singing into it and out the other side, like it used to do. Get started!'

Sam and Willie turned astonished faces up at her.

'Your wages are to be increased by five pounds a week,' cried Sophie.

Then she ran along the corridor to another room that had

been in silent mourning for thirty years, and let the air and the light in, and set free the lovely furniture, pictures, ornaments. She adjusted the weights in the tall bronze clock. The pendulum swung – time began again in the room.

She had to sit down and have a longer rest. The wonder of all that had happened that day had exhausted her.

An hour ago the Edinburgh lawyer had left the house, having read the will.

It was the strangest will ever read.

The memory of Miss Troll's face, at the part that concerned her, sent Sophie into another wild outburst of merriment . . . 'To Martha Troll, my companion, I leave and bequeath one pot of honey a month, in the vain hope that it may sweeten her disposition' . . .

Sophie had never seen anything so droll as the look on Miss Troll's face then! The girl rocked back and fore in the chair with laughter. She laughed till tears streamed down her cheeks.

Delight and wonderment echoed in room after room. It was hers – all hers!

The look on her mother's face had been almost as comical. 'To my cook and cleaning-woman, Mrs Sandra Birsay, as her existence seems to be devoted to the brewing of tea, I leave my best china teapot, along with half-a-dozen matching cups and saucers, so that she can make tea everlasting from this day to the day of her funeral' . . .

'That lovely teapot mine!' Mrs Birsay had cried. 'How kind!'

As for Miss Troll, after the first horrified gape at the lawyer's mouth pronouncing sentence, an extraordinary sequence of expressions had passed across her face: bewilderment, disbelief, self-pity, sorrow, rage, resignation, despair.

Sophie, going between two rooms, cried over the banister, so that the two women drinking tea in the kitchen could hear her, 'Don't worry, Miss Troll! The gate-house is yours – I'm giving it to you. You are to have fifty pounds a week pension from today on' . . .

The next room that Sophie went into was the music room . . . How beautiful it looked with the sun shining in and the rosewood piano uncovered for the first time. It was locked. Sophie found the key on the mantelpiece, under the portrait of a beautiful young woman who bore a striking resemblance to Mrs Maida as she might have looked sixty years before . . . Sophie's hand moved at random over the keyboard – ah, now she would be able to have lessons; she could well afford it! . . . The notes roused echoes all over the upper storey of the big house. There were music sheets in the piano stool, with the name 'Sunniva Maida' written in round immature script.

Sophie kissed the plaster cheek of Chopin.

Two hundred and fifty thousand, five hundred and twenty-one pounds and three pence . . . That's how much Sophie was worth, since an hour ago. 'Apart from the Hall and all the grounds and outhouses, and furnishings and objects of art and all appurtenances whatsoever belonging to the Hall, I leave and bequeath the residue of my estate to the girl Sophie Birsay: in the fair hope that, after such a long winter, she will bring April into a dead house and, after April, a long long summer filled with song, blossom, and the laughter of children, for many generations' . . .

The voice of the little lawyer, unused to such poetry in the documents he handled, had paused to say, 'The late Mrs Maida's own words . . . The residue of the estate, after the deduction of all taxes, duties, fees, and expenses, amounts to £250,521.3. In due course, a cheque for that amount will be sent to the young lady I see sitting before me.'

He had given Sophie a thin conspiratorial smile . . .

Poor Miss Troll still sat, petrified by the thunderbolt. Her mother had managed to say, 'A cup of tea will do us all a world of good' . . .

A teapot and six cups and saucers! Sophie leaned over the banister rail. 'Mother, I will get a golden teapot specially for you. I appoint you housekeeper here in the Hall. Your salary will be one hundred pounds a week . . .'

Whispers down below, in the kitchen, and the clink of cups. More tea had been brewed, obviously. There would be an ocean of tea in that kitchen before nightfall!

Sophie found herself in the room of death before she was

aware of it. Here Mrs Maida had endured the last thirty years of her life. Here, three weeks ago, she had died.

Sophie threw open the window. The gardeners, Sam and Willie, were already beginning to clear the choked burn. She could actually hear the first singing of the waters. Soon there would be a little blue lake under the sycamore tree, reflecting the birds and leaves of summer.

Sophie opened a cupboard and found bundles of letters tied with red ribbons. Someone, far back in time, had loved Mrs Maida . . .

Ah, the excitement of the day had wrung Sophie dry! As she went down the wide stairway – *her* stairway, in *her* vast house – to get a cup of tea before the teapot was dry, she heard the music from the music room: wistful, delicate, heart-breaking, yet it trembled (lingering) on the verge of an all-but-impossible promise.

Her Brother Died

George Friel

Mr Ramsay, a clerk in the offices of a Clydebank engineering firm, went to church every Sunday in a suit he wore only on that day, with a large Bible under one arm and his wife on the other. Behind them their two children, a boy and a girl, walked demurely. The mother was a small, dreamy woman, anæmic-looking, and the children were thin, with large, staring eyes.

When her husband died unexpectedly, Mrs Ramsay looked dreamier than ever, and stopped going to church. Freed from the strict supervision of their father, the boy and girl played in the backyard, where in his lifetime they had been forbidden to go because he was sure they would learn nothing good from the children there, so badly brought up that they swore, pilfered and fought, and were never taken to church. The girl was always at her brother's heels then. He was two years older than she was, and she relied on him in everything. But he was a timid leader, and when he first began to go into the yard the other children called him 'Jessie' because his sister was always with him, and jeered at his cowardice and thinness. So the boy and girl wandered round the yards, hovering silently together on the fringe of the noisy games and squabbles of the others.

After a while, the boy was allowed to enter a game occasionally, and his sister remained outside, watching him with large, docile eyes. When the game allowed it, he secured her a place in it beside the sisters of the other boys; but she had always to be on his side, or she was clumsy and nervous, ready to burst into tears if any of the children callously mocked her.

One evening in spring, when she was thirteen and grown into a shy big girl, she dallied in the backcourt with her brother after a crowded, quarrelsome game had broken up. As they played alone at ball-throwing, another boy and girl came into the yard, both between fourteen and fifteen; and seeing them, her brother leaned against the wall, as if ashamed to be seen playing in the yard at his age with his sister, disowning her and the game. But he livened to it again when the others merrily seized the ball and began to play.

The yard grew dark in the late twilight as they played on, and seeing them take possession of the ball as if it were theirs, cutting her out, the girl wanted to ask her brother to go upstairs with her, but she was afraid to open her mouth. Standing unnoticed, nervously twisting her fingers, she hated the elder girl for her restless impudence, her loud voice and her gay manner, and jealously watched her domineer the two boys.

Then their haphazard game died away, and her brother returned to her side as, whispering and laughing, the other two scuffled into the corner of the yard and wrestled against the broken paling. She wanted to go away, and glanced in confusion at her brother; but he was staring at the boy and girl embraced in the corner, his mouth hanging open in a foolish grin. Then with a mighty heave the girl pushed the boy away, and in a voice bright with boldness said: 'Try it with Mona Ramsay!'

She looked in alarm from one to the other, blushing self-consciously, when she heard her name mentioned; and turning again to her brother for support in her vague terror, she saw him move awkwardly over to the girl lolling alone in the corner, his arms reaching uncertainly forward. Hurt and humiliated at his leaving her and ashamed to see him try to embrace the laughing girl flaunting her skirts at him, she was so upset she did not see the other boy come at her side. Then suddenly she felt his arm around her, and before she could move he kissed her clumsily.

When he let her go, she ran in a panic over to the closeway out of the yard, her lower lip trembling, her face scarlet. Then she stopped there, expecting her brother to come loyally forward. But he was still in the corner, his back turned to her, and the girl was clenching his hand and so twisting his fingers that he was bent in pain, squirming to release himself. Standing alone, in an agony of confusion, she saw the other two stare at her in amusement. Her lower lip increased its trembling, and in a moment she was sobbing. Jerking round, her hand at her eyes, she ran through the close, and for the first time went upstairs alone. When her brother came in, she did not speak to him.

But from that night she began to change. She stopped depending on her brother, and jeered at him as often as she could find the slightest opportunity. His excited attempt to kiss Sadie Cameron, and the easy way that girl had twisted his fingers and kept him harmlessly off, made her look down on him. She sought to imitate that girl, joined her to be chased by boys, and remained with her in the backyard late when the children who were still at school had gone upstairs. No longer timid and silent, she delighted in teasing the youths who came near her, and found an exciting power in her new boldness. She saw she could make them as flustered and clumsy as her brother had been, and that pleased her.

When she left school and became too old to play in the yard, she went her own way at night, parading the streets till eleven o'clock with a chosen ally, walking from the Barracks to the Cross and back again, courting the approach of strange boys and then standing lingeringly with them in closeways and shop-entrances. Her big eyes gave her face a doll-like look, and she was fond of posing in front of a mirror, fingering her face and appraising it, using rouge and powder with extravagance before she was a year left school.

Between sixteen and seventeen she began to frequent dance-halls. Unruled by her feckless mother, she kept the greater part of her wages as an office girl to herself, and every week she had some new trifle to deck out her dress. She became notorious for her style, not content to be merely smart, but seeking always something outstanding, some frill or hue that would distinguish her from everybody. The gossiping matrons compared her unfavourably with Ella Vernon, who was always fashionable and yet always quiet, and righteously asked each other what the mother was thinking of, to let the girl go dancing every night in the week and be dolled up like that on the few shillings she would get in an office. They felt their dark hints and worst suspicions fully justified when, on a new film star making blond hair the symbol of passionate beauty, the girl who until then had been a dull brunette appeared proudly hatless. Her hair was a light yellow, nearly white. The unnatural splendour of it, waved and brilliant, made the neighbours sure she was on the downward path.

And all this time she was becoming more and more alien to her brother. Her behaviour shocked him, but he was afraid to speak to her. His two years seniority seemed negligible now they were both beginning to be grown up, and he felt he had no authority over her; sometimes, with a vague recollection of her childhood dependence on him, he wondered how it had come to pass that now she bossed him and lived so wilfully different from him. He worked as a clerk in a factor's office, wore his bowler hat even after office hours, and was beginning to go back to the Presbyterian church his father had attended. Pale-faced, round-shouldered and spectacled since seventeen, he was highly thought of by the gossiping matrons as a serious, steady young man, surely a help and a blessing to his mother compared with the gadabout, painted girl.

But there was an element of sympathy in the praise of the matrons, for it was rumoured that he was consumptive, and the local historians reminded the younger gossips that the father had died from consumption. It was then in pleasure and pride at having foretold it, rather than in pity at his state, that they saw him in such ill-health that he was able to attend his work only irregularly, and finally, when he was twenty-two, become so bad that he stopped working altogether and lay all day on a couch by the front-room window, looking down on the main road leading out of the city to the land of the lochs.

During his decline, his sister passed from the local dance-halls, and – becoming more and more uppish and affected in dress and voice – went to expensive resorts, often with an escort who had a two-seater car. Added to the pleasure-hunting heedlessness in his sister, isolating him completely in his illness, was an increasing uselessness in his mother. The neighbours whispered she was already in her dotage, and to help her in her double task of housework and looking after an invalid, one of the childless married women of the tenement began to go about the house. It was not purely from kindliness that she did so: she was inquisitive, with little to do in her own house, and in her boredom sought the material of gossip. Also, she had a hankering to be rude to the daughter, to constrain and rule her as she was sure she could have done with any child of her own. But the wandered mother saw only that the gratuitous interference left her undisturbed in her sorrowful weariness and took out of her hands tasks she could never have finished without getting into a muddle. So two or three times a day she would say to the bustling, meddlesome neighbour: 'I don't know what I'd do without you, Mrs Hamilton.'

After a long illness, the young man died at three o'clock in a May morning, and Mrs Hamilton took brusque control. It was a situation perfectly suited to her talents. She pulled down the blinds, sent for the undertaker, arranged for the burial, organized a subscription among the neighbours to buy flowers for the coffin, and saw to the insurance money. Looking blank, and quite helpless in her grief, the mother did not even know what was being done. She clung to her daughter and wept in brief but frequent spasms, little trickles of tears running down her vacuous face, while her trembling hand tightly held a small handkerchief which she could not even raise to her eyes. And supporting her mother in their loss, the girl suddenly broke down and wailed for half an hour. But, after that she was dry-eyed again, and simply looked absent-minded. Yet her evidence of sorrow softened Mrs Hamilton's hostility, and it was retailed immediately to the gossip-hungry neighbours. They interpreted it magnanimously, heads sympathetically nodding, as proof that the girl was not really bad at heart, but just flighty and empty-headed. And the eldest of them, looking back into the past with an expression of pathos at the transience of youth and human affection, recalled that the boy and girl had been inseparable as children. Then there was elaborated the tale of a sisterly love, deep, constant, and hidden, and every one was sorry for the girl who had suffered the great loss of her only brother, the only one she ever cared for. The mother, it was said, fortunately didn't realize what had happened.

Mrs Hamilton arranged the funeral for three o'clock the next afternoon, and lived in the Ramsays' house till then, attending to the prostrate mother and the mute girl. She tidied the kitchen in the morning, had the coffin with the body laid out in the front-room, and set out an abundance of wreaths and bouquets there, beaming with pride at the success of her subscription list.

Early in the afternoon she sat in the kitchen talking to the mother, trying, as she said later, to distract the poor woman. Wearing a black dress, her face pale and washed-out looking, the girl sat away from them with her elbow on her knee and her head on her hand. Then she rose quietly and went through to the front-room where the coffin and all the flowers were. The only sound in the darkened house was Mrs Hamilton's prattling. Occasionally she stopped talking, hoping in her tender sympathy to hear the girl weeping in the next room. But when she stopped talking the whole world seemed silent. Then as it came near the hour when the neighbours going with the carriages should come in, she rose and went through the lobby, moving with reverent quietness, to fetch the girl to the kitchen in readiness to receive the visitors. The door of the front-room was closed, and with self-conscious tact she softly opened it and peeped in sympathetically. Her head jerked convulsively in astonishment, and her hand tightened on the door-knob to support her as she craned incredulously forward.

The room was dim in the twilight caused by the drawn blinds, and on the table in the centre of it lay the lidded coffin. But there were no flowers on it or round it or near it. In front of the wardrobe mirror, her black dress changed for a long-skirted, turquoise-blue dance frock that showed up her bosom and hips, the girl swayed and pirouetted and posed. One of the wreaths was round her neck, a single red flower was in her glaring blond hair, and in each hand she held a large bouquet. Other wreaths and bouquets were strewn symmetrically on the carpet at her feet, and when she swayed with her back to the large mirror, her arms slowly flapping, she looked thoughtfully over her shoulder, studying her pose. Then pirouetting again, bending her torso back, she tried another one, obliquely appraising herself garlanded, picking out a languid waltz between the scattered flowers on the floor.

Old Wives' Tales

Wilma Murray

That, kiddo, was called a contraction. No doubt about it now.

So. This is it, then.

It's just you and me now. Till birth us do part.

Don't get scared. I reckon we have a few hours left to ourselves before we have to tell anyone. And I need the time. Okay? You see, while the world is turning ever so casually on its axis, I am about to be slipped into a supporting role for the rest of my life to leave you the centre stage. It may be the first day of your life, but it's the last day of my childhood. So give me a few hours to get used to the idea, eh?

That sounds selfish. I know. But don't fret. There'll be years and years ahead for me to worry about you.

I must say you haven't got much of a day for it. In fact, if I were at all superstitious and chose to believe the omens like grandma did, I can tell you they're not good. The sun's not even shining. There's a distinct smell of withering in the air this grey September morning. See, the roses are rotted with the rain and it looks like every pest in the book is busy chewing holes and spitting green. At least Fat-Cat's pleased. They've cut the barley and all the refugee mice have taken him completely by surprise this morning. He'll come in and present us with another little furry body in some advanced state of shock any time now. Stay where you are for a while. Have a last swim around in the warm dark. There's nothing out here for you today. No star in the east or three wise men for you, kiddo.

Funny how I thought I'd be ready for all this. Just a few more hours. Please? If you don't panic, I won't. But it's not how it was described in the manual.

Aww . . . Jesus! Okay, okay. I'll see if I can get you one wise woman.

I told you. The world out here's not a place to rush into.

There's AIDS, drugs and God knows what all lurking out here, colds and rotten teeth, acid rain and nuclear waste – all this in spite of the wonder of the modern world. (They can predict the return of Halley's comet with pinpoint accuracy, but they couldn't tell me when you would be born. Doesn't that seem odd to you?)

What else can I tell you about your chosen birth day, then? Well, Nelson Mandela is *still* in prison, there are killings in Northern Ireland, wars in three continents, famine in another, but, Coronation, Street carries on. Women are spying on Greenham Common and picking brambles at the same time, pinning hopes on wholesome pies and laying down a future in jams and good strong wine. Just wait till you taste a bramble and apple pie!

It's a funny old world. And don't you go expecting me to explain it all away, either. I'll wipe your bum and put plasters on your knees, maybe teach you to play the piano and help you with your homework. After that, you're on your own, kiddo. Like the rest of us. Mummies can't kiss the world better any more and there ain't no fairy godmothers.

There are grandmas, though. They're the next best thing. They're good with the fairy tales, are grandmas. I have one of my own, so I know. Of course, you'll be seeing her soon. She's something else, that one. When I asked her – you know, woman to woman for the very first time – what it was like the day mother was born, she told me it was snowing! The omens seemed good for the times, she said. It was Winston Churchill's birthday and St Andrew's Day, so the flags were flying. Well, you had to keep your spirits up during the war, she said. She would tell my mother the flags were up for her and not worry her about things like war.

You could keep them ignorant then, you see. No TV. Anyway, she told me all of that, almost in one breath, but did not volunteer one word about the birth itself. She remembers the midwife's jokes and her bad feet, though. She patted my arm finally and said I'd forget about it as soon as it was over. That was a great help. And mother, she still can't bear to watch war documentaries or read about the Holocaust because she knows she spent the whole sorry six years skipping through other people's time. I teased her about grandma telling her the flags were for her and she gave me that look. The one that can tidy up a room.

Not that she was any great help either. When I asked her what it was like the day I was born, she said it was a scorcher and she just about died of thirst. My God! I should have thought that was the least of her problems. I persisted, but it's not easy asking your mother little questions like – how was your labour? She told me it took twenty-eight hours and the temperature outside rose to eighty at one point. Some kids at the local school sports collapsed with heatstroke, she remembers. I wasn't asking about the weather, dammit.

If you're a girl, I promise, I do, I promise that when the time comes I'll tell you every last detail. Come to think of it, I'll tell you even if you're a boy. I'm all for equality.

In the end, she confided it wasn't too bad. Anyway, she said, it'll all be worth it. And that's it. That's the extent of the experience handed down through generations to me, now, with my big belly.

Hey! Is this hurting you as much as it's hurting me? Read the book, kiddo. This is supposed to be the good bit. So hang on to your hat, because here it comes again.

Holy. Hell!

I knew it. I just knew it. She was lying through her teeth. Twenty-eight hours she was in labour with me. Twenty-eight hours! And all she'll tell me is that it wasn't too bad. So what's bad? What are we registering on the Richter scale now, for example? I tell you, this is getting scary.

Where's that book?

Where's that bloody book?

Recite something, the book says. Quick.

> *Humpty Dumpty sat on a wall*
> *Humpty Dumpty had a great fall*
> *All the King's horses*

And all the King's men
Couldn't put Humpty together again.

That's going to go down well in the ambulance. Speaking of which, I'm going to phone them. Sorry, but I'm losing my grip, as they say, and it's your fault.

No, forgive me. That's not true. It's their fault. The secret society of mothers out there.

You okay in there? Just hold on a while yet, kiddo. Hey! I'll soon have to stop calling you that. You'll have a name. And all the other trappings of a statistic. They'll start a file on you and you'll get orange juice, an education and free dental treatment till you're sixteen. Then you'll get to collect Social Security like the rest of us. Just like your Dad. And if you're wondering where your other parent is at this critical juncture in your life, he's out looking for work, again. That's where he is. I sent him off this morning without telling him about the queer ache in my back that started all this. Well, he would only have fussed. He's a lovely man, though. You'll like him. I promise. But if he doesn't find a job soon, you'll have that on your birth certificate, you know. Father – Unemployed.

This is not funny any more. I'm not sure I can take much more of it. WHY DIDN'T SOMEONE TELL ME?

Humpty Dumpty sat on a wall
Humpty Dumpty had a great fall . . .

Myself, I think he was conned. Just like me. Why else would an egg go and jump off a wall? Well, there's a lot of it about. I suppose. Conspiracy, that is. I did warn you it wasn't much of a world. Everybody's at it. Governments, drug companies, slimming magazines and that silly bitch who ran the antenatal classes. To think I believed all that guff about clenched fists mimicking contractions.

Remember? 'Tighten. Clench. Ho-o-ld it. Re-lax.' What a load of crap.

Just like mother and her 'not too bad'. Just like all of them, all the bloody mothers down all the bloody generations who have never told it as it is. THANK YOU FOR NOTHING ALL YOU MOTHERS OUT THERE.

Oh, but it will all be worth it, they say.

Oh? Will it really?

You'll forget about it as soon as it's over, they say.

No I won't. I'm going to spill the beans. I'm going to tell all. And I'm telling you, kiddo. This is hell.

This. This is the biggest con of them all. This is the lulu. This ... Oh, God ... I bet if someone asked the Virgin Mary what it was like the day Jesus was born, she'd say it was a fine clear night with plenty of stars.

I wonder if Jesus had a birth certificate? Father – God. Hah! Imagine trying to get that through the system today.

INPUT ERROR.

PLEASE RETYPE.

Don't worry, kiddo. You don't have a God in the family. You won't upset any of their computer programmes.

> *Humpty Dumpty sat on a wall*
> *Humpty Dumpty had a great fall*
> *All the King's horses and all the King's men*
> *Couldn't put Humpty together again.*

It has not escaped my notice how much I resemble an egg.

So.

It's time to go, kiddo.

Let's go jump off the wall.

Remember Me

Naomi Mitchison

My name is Jessie MacKinnon. I was on the District Council for
ten years and since then on the Community Council; I was Vice-
Chairman, and indeed I am acting Chairman now. There was
this and that committee and group in our small community a few
miles out from Oban. My husband had a small mixed farm,
which did well enough and gave him plenty of time in the winter
for reading and wood-work. He was a great reader. After he died
I carried on working the farm with one old man, for I liked doing
it, but Rob and Sandy used to come out with their families and
help me in holiday times. Sometimes in summer I used to let to a
few boarders, nice folk. They came back mostly, I remember;
they were all terribly taken with my garden, all of them, and the
view. I had children. I had friends. It is all past.

My little granddaughter Fiona was staying with me, Rob and
Mary's youngest. It is because of her that it is at all worth my
while to be alive, and sometimes looking at her I wonder. For I ask
myself has she truly escaped? She is beginning to grow up, to
have the thoughts that come naturally to a young girl. But then?
At least she looks better than most of the other children. Better
indeed than some of them, poor wee mites.

This is the way it was with me. It was a light west wind and I was
out in my garden, looking into the wind, so that I never saw the
flash east over Glasgow. I only – somehow knew that something
had happened. I turned and I saw the cloud go up. Then
another. I thought about Rob and Mary; well, I will not speak of
that now, nor of much else. My other son was in the Midlands of
England: himself and – all of them. No word has come through.
Nor will it now.

Queer things went through my head. The old man who helps
on the farm, Colin Mor, came over from the sheds. He said,
'They have done it,' and then he stared round and began

muttering about would the pensions go on. I looked at him and it changed to some kind of prayer. And then it was one of my neighbours, Miss Paterson, who had the rockery with the fancy heaths and the gentians. She watched the cloud with me and I felt her hand on my arm. She said, in a shaky voice, 'No more Strathclyde now, Jessie.' You see, we had all been speaking together about the new local government set-up and how badly it was turning out for us on the fringes, and then we both looked at one another and I knew she had said that in the hope of taking my mind off what she knew it must be on. And with that I remembered how she had a sister and brother-in-law in Helensburgh. So some way we managed a small laugh, and then I said, 'We'd best get down to Connel.' That was the Civil Defence Centre by the loch, and we had both said we would go over and help if there was ever any need, though some way we thought there never would be. We could not have brought ourselves to think otherwise. They had a stock of medicines and blankets and all that down there. She said hesitating, 'Have you tried the phone?' I said no, for I knew, I knew. But yet now she had said it I lifted the receiver and dialled the number I knew so well. But there was nothing, nothing at all.

I gave Fiona a book and some sweeties and a great petting, saying I'd be gone for a while. She had not noticed a thing, indoors. I told her I would lock the door in case bad people were to come, but it was mostly to stop her going out – and touching anything. The flowers were still blooming, but if the wind changed –

We drove down to Connel and even then I began to wonder about petrol. We waited with others. Some of us tried to reason out why it had happened. The laird's wife said they had been small bombs or rockets, if it had been one of the big ones we would all be dead. 'Theatre weapons,' she said and somehow naming it made it less terrible. One could hold it in the mind then. But the thing was, we had thought we were out of the world danger, that a small country such as we are today need not be drawn in. We did not know then what was being done over our heads. I am not even clear today, for the news that gets through is not to be trusted. No more than one can trust the grass or the sky. Not any more.

It was on into evening before the first of the buses got through, and then the rest, and I looking, looking for my own ones. Just in case. It was not until a week or two after when they began to die that I could bring myself to be glad that Rob and Mary and Andy and Jean had not been among them; that it was all over for them, almost before I had seen the cloud. The only train that got through had been standing at Garelochhead; the driver was burned, but he carried on, the decent man; I remember he did not die for quite a while. He lifted a load all up from there to Arrochar; the woods were all on fire round him; it was the ones who had been working their gardens or that who had the burns. No train from further down Loch Long had a chance. The ones who came on the buses were from Alexandria and Balloch, the western edge of Dumbarton even. There were a few from Helensburgh who got across to the Lomond side-road, but they had been badly caught by the Holy Loch bomb. They had the most terrible things to tell us; some of them seemed to be going to live, but they had these burns that did not heal. The blankets were mostly used to bury them in. That is, until we began to see that there would be no more blankets and we could not afford to let the dead have any of them. The laird's wife brought down stuff from the Big House. Their son and his family were in Australia; they had not heard yet when I saw them last, and if the son were ever to get here, what would he find?

Miss Paterson had given up hope for her sister and brother-in-law. She was working hard, wearing herself out. I could see how Dr Bowles was counting on her; he was an elderly man who had come out to the highlands mainly for the fishing and golf and the pleasure of it here, as it was in those days. He had read the leaflets but had barely taken them in. The young doctor from Oban, Dr MacAndrew, knew more. But I could see how even he flinched from the burns. It was later that Miss Paterson told me about how hard it was to forget that her sister had a baby coming, her first. There were wee coats and socks that Elsie Paterson had been knitting, put away in tissue paper. For weeks after she kept dreaming she was putting another one away in the press. And then she woke. Those were the kind of dreams I had too.

That first night the wind blew itself out and there was a calm. But even while it seemed to be blowing there must have been a current away above us that was bringing some of the evil stuff west and over. I have some sense and I kept Fiona in the house, but myself I was working for the refugees. The District Nurse was on leave. She never came back. I started by bringing all my milk over to the centre; I thought it was the best way I could help. Dr Bowles had been pleased at first, but young Dr MacAndrew – he is dead now but he was a fine young man – said to me that it was as good as poisoned. 'Throw it away!' he said, and he told me quick while he was dressing a burn, for we still had dressings in those days, that the milk would be full of radioactive iodine and must on no account be given to anyone, above all not a child. It could damage the child's thyroid gland and give it a cancer or turn it into an idiot.

We all know that now. Too well do we know it. But then it was news and not everyone believed. Dr MacAndrew said to me, 'Go round to your neighbours, Mrs MacKinnon, and warn them every one, and above all those with bairns. And mind, not a drop to Fiona.' So I did just that, but half of them laughed at me; it seemed against nature that good milk with nothing at all wrong in the look of it could hurt a child. So it came about that before a year had passed I saw my nearest neighbour's three turning from lively bright children into listless miseries. One of them has just died; we all know that is best.

Yet at the time it seemed just crazy; Fiona had been with me just because she'd had the measles and was needing good food. I did not think to do this extra washing of the vegetables which I do, not until later. Even so it had me puzzled, for we get our water from the high loch and it would be bound to get as much fall-out as the grass. I had not thought it out; when I did I began drawing water out of the old well, that is fed by a spring from far underground. I look and look at Fiona and wonder, did I keep enough of the stuff away from her? Or will she have something secretly eating at her? It is, I suppose, probable that she escaped. But I cannot help thinking sometimes that I did not do enough.

I have even tried to pray for Fiona, but I just cannot get myself to believe that it is any use now. I don't know even how she has taken it all. She clings onto me, but not too badly. She never or hardly ever speaks of what has been. Only at birthday or Christmas time. Mostly she tries to take the burden off me, more perhaps than a child her age should do.

I had of course to tell her, but not until we were totally certain, beyond the reach of any hope. I think she knew by then. She asked about her uncle Sandy and the cousins, down south. Betty was her own age. I said we should not hope too much. By that time we had come to the conclusion that a string of these rocket bombs had been targetted across all the industrial parts of Scotland and England. Strategic destruction that is called. Not murder.

The police came over with their geiger counters, walking about the fields and houses. After a time they said it was safe or just about. 'Not like nearer in' I mind they said. One or two had been as far as Inveraray and they say the things ticked away there. Over the Rest they did not go. Nobody did. Arrochar – it is just a name now. But, for all they said, I found it hard to believe that our own land was unhurt.

Gradually we got a drift in of survivors, not like the first lot, though some had small burns or radiation sickness which did not kill at once; some of these have survived. But most were people who came where they thought there would be food. Some had their living knocked away. Some had been staying in hotels, though the full tourist season had not been on when the thing happened. The hotels shut and the guests had no way of going back to wherever they had come from; they were cut off except from the west. They drove as far as their petrol would take them and offered money, but what was the use of that? Still and all, those of us like myself who had rooms, took them in if they seemed decent. I had first an old lady and got mortally tired of her; she did nothing but complain. Then I took in an Edinburgh couple with two small children; I thought Fiona might like them.

Mr Drummond did not look strong; he had been in some kind of an office with good pay; he seemed to think that some day he'd be back and find it going on. Indeed he tried to bluster at first and sell me his car for a great price, but his wife had more sense and we got together.

She would help with the housework and cooking, but she turned out to be a poor cook, having only done it in a town. He would dig, help on the farm and so on. I thought, well, he could dig up the back part of my garden behind the dyke which I had not bothered about for long enough, and we would put in more vegetable seeds. He agreed. We went to Oban together and got plenty of seeds. The shops still took money, in hope, one supposes, that some day it would be worth something. He did not know much about gardening but came back with a heavy spade and fork, and he certainly worked and did not complain about his blisters or the nettle stings. But we did not see much of each other.

They were in what had been Rob and Mary's room. I would wake in the night and hear them moving and for seconds, until my mind cleared, I would have the warm feeling that they were mine, not these strangers. I was not the only one to have that feeling about the Incomers.

Yet in a way it was worse for them, since they had lost everything, while we still had our homes. I knew that and yet I could not be welcoming. So they were apt to get together and let out to one another how they felt about us. One can get the feel of this kind of thing in a small community and we could not blame them. But more had gone on to Oban and even to the islands and Ardnamurchan. And one or two had skills we needed; there is a brisk wee dressmaker from up Stirling way who never seems short of eggs or potatoes or even flowers.

Looking back on last year I find it hard some way to remember just when things happened. The electricity still goes on sometimes and was good enough for a while, since most of the hydro-electric stations were far enough from the towns. The others, the coal-fired ones, were put out of action at once. They say the great building at Longannet is still standing and the turbines inside it. Some day perhaps it will be possible for people to go back into it, start it all up again. Not in my time, nor yet Fiona's. But the Falkirk bomb destroyed most of the works and until we can build up some kind of industry in Scotland there's power to spare. But things go wrong at our own sub-station level and there is no way of getting repairs. Some of the men have gone into the outskirts for short times and tried to get what supplies and spares they could carry away in barrows. But it is terribly risky, even with rubber boots and gloves. We would never urge anyone to do it.

It stands to reason that there was no petrol after the first month, even with the hard rationing. There was fighting over the last of it in Oban, and two of the police badly hurt. Perhaps this was to be expected. Here we just accepted it decently. But I'm wondering how long my poor old pony will last; he had to eat the grass and it must have been thick with fall-out. For that matter, even if the wind had not changed, the stuff would have got back to us right round the world. As it must have come to everyone everywhere, even those who sent out the planes: but not strongly – I could wish it had been. We all worry about our beasts; I gave the first milk to the calves and they are not looking too grand for yearling queys and stots. The milk should be safe now with the radioactive iodine worn off and I could wish I had more of it, but the cows are just not in calf. We are hoping it will wear off as the ones with the geiger counters say, and it is great news when we hear of a new calf, even if it may be a bitty misshapen. But some of us small farmers depended on the A.I. centre with the stuff driven out to us, and that had to close down at once; it is queer how much we took for granted in the old days, now we are back to something much older. Maybe this summer when the flush of grass is on I shall be able to make a bit butter; it is something one misses, and Mrs Drummond seemed to think there'd be bound to be margarine at least, in the shops. Some of the folk with big deep-freezes and the Oban hotels themselves bought it up, but some of this was lost when the electricity went off, and the rest of us were not sorry for them.

It was the same going back to old ways with the fishing and all the boats depending on diesel, not just the engines but the winches and every new bit of machinery. The nets they had were far and away too heavy to haul by hand. But the fishermen got going, I'll say that for them; the big boats are laid up, but the small ones are out with lines and lobster pots and their trawl nets cut up into something lighter. It's the queerest thing, but already there seem to be more fish coming back; I have dried and salted a few. Yet I am doubtful about some of them. I remember Dr MacAndrew saying to a meeting of housewives, 'It is this stuff the herring feed on, the plankton, that gets hold of the radioactive material that has fallen into the water, and it stands to reason the herring will be full of it, and so will the mackerel.' Yes, I remember that day well, for soon after that he got ill himself and knew there was nothing to be done. He had gone as far as Crianlarich to try to help the doctor there and both of them had gone down with the radiation sickness. I used to go over and sit with him once in a while. He would not go into hospital. It was crowded out and he said to me, 'We mustn't waste resources. Remember that, Mrs MacKinnon.' His voice had gone thin by then, and he was vomiting now and again; I wiped his face for him and he was saying he was sorry and trying to smile.

Yes, I have remembered. We have to make do with our own food. The tins in the shops are all done, even the kinds one never used to buy. I am lucky that my hens are still laying. Nearer Glasgow most of the poultry as well as the cattle died. They say there is hardly a cattle beast left in Dalmally and Tyndrum, as well as Strachur way. South of Tarbert there is nothing alive. One of the things had been targetted on Macrihanish. It was hard somehow the way we in western Scotland had been loaded up with these things which have brought destruction down on us and we were never even consulted. Defence, they said! When the haze came creeping over everything and the whole eastern sky glared like hellmouth – some way I had expected this – I kept in all the beasts from the inbye land and the hens, just as I kept in Fiona. I mind now I slapped her for running out. My heart bleeds for it but I know I was right. But the way I was placed I could not get the sheep from the high ground – indeed we had nowhere to put them under cover, none of us – and things have gone badly there. We would find a dead sheep here or there and when it came to lambing time, there were dead lambs and sick ewes. It is the same for all of us.

Maybe all this worrying about what we shall have to eat and to wear and how to mend our houses is some help against the deep grief which we almost all have and the feeling night and day that we are cut off. The telly went blank, though for a time some people kept trying it; they just couldn't believe it was over for ever. My radio never got much beyond Radio Scotland and Clyde. But I kept on trying. Once or twice I have heard foreign voices; I thought I could even make out a bit of French once, but it was faint and I could not get anything from it. Yet there are other people, maybe in the same fix as ourselves. If once we could get to them! But how? Fiona found an old newspaper at the bottom of a press and read the big headings, the football and all that. Finished. Finished. Then she found the strip cartoons and she was at me to know what happened next, so we made up stories. But I was glad to burn that newspaper and all the cheery lies it had in it. I can remember that it used to be said by the Americans and the Russians and the Chinese that they could stand an atomic war because it would only kill one in three or maybe one in four of their populations. I do not care one bit if there are no Americans left or no Russians or no Chinese. I would not lift one finger to help any of them if I saw one in trouble. Yet once I was a good church member with a great belief in human brotherhood. It is as though love has been killed in me.

Some of the folk round here have been going to the church and seem to be all the better for an hour of hymn-singing. But not me. I went once and the Minister kept on about sin and how we were being punished. But it seemed to me that all he had in mind was the wee kind of sins, gambling and fornication and drink. And the sins that brought all this on us were of a different kind altogether and nothing to do with God looking on to see if the boys were playing cards for money at the back of a haystack.

We brought it on ourselves. It was not God. Without our intending it surely, but that made no difference.

At first we tried to go on with local government as it was. But it was too difficult. We had too much to do, all of us, and the Strathclyde administration was finished as though it had never been and the District Council could not go on. For a while we telephoned to Lochgilphead, but then the lines went down in a storm that November and could not be repaired. Even in Lochgilphead there were some people burned and a terrible lot of sickness later. The hospital there was to receive casualties from Glasgow; some got through, but most were scared of heading south again; it was too near the Holy Loch. I don't know how they got on later. Nobody has been that far for months, though we might manage it maybe next year. The District Engineer that we used to see at the Oban meetings tried to get through to Dunoon. He was a brave man, but it is just not enough to be brave. He is dead.

But when it comes to the bit, local government, whatever you call it, depends on grants from the central government. And there is no government. There is no centre. Schools only go on because we, the parents and grandparents, pay the teachers in eggs or potatoes, peats or meal. I gave one of them a box my husband had made; it had a lock and key. That matters these days. Public health is gradually breaking down for want of equipment. One of the married District Nurses who had retired came on again when it was clear that our own nurse would never come back from her leave. She had us all out gathering sphagnum moss and drying it for dressings and for use when there were no more sanitary towels to be had. We need to think of everything.

There is no postal service with no petrol for the vans. And I will never get the letters I used to look for. Never. Never. But our old Postie got hold of a pony and starting running a service on his own, in and out of Oban, with the odd passenger and letter or parcel. He says that it's happening in north and mid-Argyll, and indeed we are beginning to get in touch, though everything is gone beyond Ballachulish. It must have been

Inverness and Fort William that they picked out. Postie sends in the bill himself, using up the old forms and saying what he will take instead of pounds. There are still a few people who use the old money. But it is little used compared with things, most of all food, and that is how we pay Postie.

Well then, it seemed to Miss Paterson and me that we should at least get the Community Council started up again, so we called a meeting, just going round. The Chairman himself had been away at the time and, well, he never came back. So it was myself that needed to take the decision. So far we have had three meetings. It is not much more than six or seven miles for anyone to come in and up to now we have managed to give the executive committee a cup of tea, but they must bring their own sugar. There had been some thefts already, so we asked the policeman to come. Things were awkward for him because he had carried out the emergency orders, but then they had stopped. Oban Headquarters was not much better off, and there had already been some crimes there, the real thing I mean, not just young people showing off. Our own policeman came in and told me they were going out armed now in Oban, but for himself he could not see himself doing anything of the kind, for after all we were all decent folk.

I was taking the meeting and maybe I saw a bitty further ahead. Anyway I proposed from the Chair that our Police Force representative should be asked in the name of the community to go out armed. It has turned out to be just as well, though there was only the one time he has had to shoot – so far. He was upset about it himself, although he missed; but the gang were scared and ran, and it has kept certain ones away. The laird's wife brought in the gun, with her husband's compliments, and he would have come himself if he had felt able. Postie went over later and asked if he could have the pair to it. I believe he has had to use it, though he will not say.

Old Dr Bowles came to the meeting, and I kept thinking if only it could have been Dr MacAndrew, for the old man was flustered and seemed some way unable to think ahead. He kept saying we ought to get in supplies, vaccines and antibiotics and that, though he knew as well as the rest of us that this was nothing but speaking into the wind. I had bought bottles of aspirin and cough mixture and disinfectant before the Oban chemist I mostly went to was out of them. The shop is shut now, and so are most of the others in Oban. I wish now I had got more sugar, but I did not wish to appear grasping; most of it has gone already, though it is nice to see the jam and jelly I have. The laird has diabetes and there is no more insulin; it is weeks now since I have seen either of them. I had not wanted to ask the Minister to the meeting, but he came and started in about sin. I told him he was out of order, and a fair few laughed.

The incomers came to the meeting and mostly sat by themselves in the two back rows, except for the dressmaker body who sat with friends near the front. They wanted a piece of land ploughed up for themselves and one of the farmers who has a pair of good horses offered to plough and harrow around an acre for them, free. But they must get their own seeds. It seemed fair enough to the rest of us, though clearly some of them thought they could do with more. They are managing with seeds this year and so are we all, but next year? Oats and barley will go on, and potatoes, but our turnips and field carrots will scarcely ripen seed so far north and I cannot see most of the greens doing it, still less the beans and peas.

The talk at the meeting, which used in the old days to be about the footpath to the school and danger from cars, or else about the bus time tables, was now about food and security from raiders and what was happening elsewhere. Postie was good and offered to find out where the rest of the Community Councils were getting together. Indeed he has done just that and maybe it will be possible to build something up. It could be the only way. We have even had a representative coming from north Argyll across the loch and we hope to send someone over to mid-Argyll. We hear from the fishermen that there have been troubles in Mull and the folk in the big hotel waving money about and trying to get hold of a plane, but we will face that when it comes. Meanwhile we will strengthen ourselves. Several of our young folk have got out their old saddles and are keen enough to ride to a meeting. They have been making bows and arrows, even. But most of the time we needed to talk about getting together for this and that which had to be done urgently. I suppose it will be like this all over wherever people have escaped and maybe we are luckier than some.

The old Oban Town Council, that was there before Strathclyde, had got together, such as were left of them, and they sent over, trying to rope us in, with talk of rating the district and that. But they had little to offer us, except for office space and acres of paper and clips and rubber bands, and it was clear that what they wanted from us would be oatmeal and mutton. So we decided to write back a polite and formal letter, but to let it be known we would not be playing their game.

It was clear to all of us that we'd need to go back to the old ways for the harvesting. A few of us had a bit of diesel oil laid by for the tractors, and some used it for harvesting, making out that something would happen one day, some help was bound to come. But it seemed to me that I would keep the little I had for the winter ploughing. My pony is not up to it. I slept with the key of the padlock under my pillow and I let it get about that I had a gun; who would know that I only have five cartridges? Though there was a time not so long ago when one could leave one's house door unlocked and no thought of harm.

Colin Mor has been terrible at first, asking for this or that, even if he knew I had none of it, but now he has settled in and is working hard. The queer thing was he wanted to keep getting his wages in cash. I told him that money was not worth having, but if that was what he wanted it suited me. I drew out all I had in my account, and borrowed quickly against my shares, though nobody, least of all the bank manager, knows if they will ever be worth anything again. But Colin Mor was happy, putting it away wherever it is he does put it, under his mattress maybe, and he was with us for harvest. He snares an odd rabbit and I make a stew with my onions and give him his share. The Drummonds did not like it at first, but they soon got over that. All of us got together when it came to a fine spell in September, and cut the oats with scythes and bound by hand; I tried to wear gloves at first, but they hinder one and we had to be quick; now I am worried about the skin on my right forefinger.

What we could not harvest at the back-end was fed to the beasts, though we were careful to keep plenty of seed. There may be enough fertilizer in the stores for next year's grain and grass, but it will need to be shared and not let the big farmers, least of all the ones in Mull, get too much of a share of it. By now we had almost forgotten which field was whose; we were needing to think all together. Again we needed to thresh by hand, since there was no fuel for the big thresher. But it is easy enough to make a flail, though hard and slow work using one. We had to grind the grain as best we could. I had a hand coffee mill and Fiona does half an hour at it after school. We were speaking at the last Community Council meeting about the possibility of getting one of the old water mills somewhere in Argyll working again. We were well aware by now that there would be no flour coming in and we must depend on our own oatmeal and barley meal. It is queer to think how little one used to value a loaf of bread.

We dug the potatoes with graips as we could not use the tractor spinners, all getting together as in the old days. Not one wee potato did we miss! We had a good feeling that they at least would be safe, though how can we be sure, for the evil stuff works down into the soil. We would find dead worms here and there. But we notice that there are far too many grubs and caterpillars and such and not the birds that used to clear them off for us. For the poor birds that were flying about in the air while it was at its worst dropped and died: it was sad to see that. One is glad of a sparrow now even. I wonder will the swallows ever come back.

I do not know how long we can go on. For the first year we still had some stores; I even made a Christmas cake for Fiona and a few other of the young ones. I used the last bit of margarine that I had been saving up and Mrs Drummond managed to find some sugar; there was a brooch she used to wear and I think that is how it went. But it started Fiona onto speaking about her last Christmas and all the fun and happiness they'd had together.

We have kept hoping that a ship might come in from somewhere. But it never does. And our health is going down. I have sore places on my insteps and my face, and my hair has fallen out in patches. There was a time I would have minded about that. Now I only mind anything because of Fiona. Yes, and the Community Council. But it is too soon to know what will happen either to the Community Council or to the children. Perhaps when we do know it will seem that we were still happy when we did not know.

Allergy

Elspeth Davie

The new lodger glanced down briefly at the plate which had just been put in front of him and turned towards the window with a faint smile, as though acknowledging that the day was fair enough outside, even if there was something foul within.

'I can't take egg. Sorry.'

'Can't take?' Mrs Ella MacLean still kept her thumb on the oozy edge of a heap of scrambled yellow.

'No. It's an allergy.'

'It doesn't agree?'

'No. It's an allergy.'

'Oh, one of those. That's interesting! But you could take a lightly-boiled egg, couldn't you?'

'No, it's an allergy to egg.'

'You mean *any* egg?'

'Any and every egg, Mrs MacLean. In all forms. Egg is poison to me.' Harry Veitch did not raise his voice at all, but this time his landlady withdrew the plate rather quickly. She put it on one side and sat down at the other end of the table.

'Yes, that *is* interesting,' she said. 'I've known the strawberries and the shellfish and the cat's fur. And of course I've heard of the egg, though I've never met it.' Veitch said nothing. He broke a piece of toast. 'No I've never met it. Though I've met eggs disagreeing. I mean really disagreeing!'

Veitch was pressing his lips with a napkin. 'Not the same thing,' he said. 'When I say poison I mean poison. Pains. Vomiting. And I wouldn't like to say what else. Violent! Not many people understand just *how* violent!'

Flickers of curiosity alternated with prim blankness in Mrs MacLean's eyes. 'And aren't there dusts and pollens – horse's hair and that sort of thing?'

'All kinds. I don't even know the lot. But they're not all as *violent.*'

There was a silence while Mrs MacLean with a soft white napkin gently, gently brushed away the scratchy toast-crumbs which lay between them in the centre of the table.

'Do you find people sympathetic then?' she enquired at last.

Veitch gave a short laugh. 'Mrs MacLean – when, may I ask, have people ever been sympathetic to anything out of the ordinary?'

'I suppose that's true.'

They both turned their heads to look out onto the Edinburgh street, already crowded with people going to work. There was a stiffish breeze – visitors from the south, like Veitch, used the word 'gale' – and those going eastwards had their teeth bared against it and their eyes screwed up in a grimace which made them appear very unsympathetic indeed. On the pavement below their window, a well-dressed man stooped in the swirling dust to unwind a strip of paper which had wrapped itself round his ankle like a dirty bandage. They heard his curse even with the window shut. This sudden glimpse of the cruelly grimacing human beings, separated from them only by glass, gave them a stronger sense of the warmth within. Human sympathy too. Mrs MacLean was a widow. It was a street of widows – some of them old and grim, living at street level between lace curtains and brown pots of creeping plants, some of them young and gay behind high window boxes where the hardiest flowers survived the Scottish summer. Mrs MacLean was neither of these. She was an amiable woman in her middle years, and lately she had begun to wonder whether sympathy was not her strongest point.

In the weeks that followed Veitch's status changed from lodger to paying guest, from paying guest, by a more subtle transformation shown only in Mrs MacLean's softer expression and tone of voice, to a guest who, in the long run, paid. They talked together in the mornings and evenings. Sometimes they talked about his work which was in the refrigerating business. But as often as not the conversation veered round to eggs. As a subject the egg had everything. It was brilliantly self-contained and clean, light but meaty, delicate yet full of complex far-reaching associations – psychological, sexual, physiological, philosophical. There was almost nothing on earth that did not start off with an egg in some shape or form. And when they had discussed eggs in the abstract Veitch would tell her about all those persons who had tried their best to poison him, coming after him with their great home-made cakes rich with egg, boggy egg puddings nourishing to the death, or the stiff drifts of meringue topping custards yellow as cowslip. It was all meant kindly, no doubt, yet how could one be sure? After all, he'd never made any secret of it. But people who called themselves human were continually dropping eggs here and there into his life as deliberately as anarchists depositing eggs of explosive into unsuspecting communities.

'You'd be amazed,' he said. 'Even persons who profess to love one aren't above mixing in the odd egg – just to test, just to make absolutely certain one isn't trying it on.'

'Oh heavens – Oh no!' cried Mrs MacLean. 'Love! Love in one hand and poison in the other!'

'That's just about it,' Veitch agreed. 'With my chemical make-up you get to know a lot about human nature, and sometimes the things you learn you'd far, far rather never have known.'

By early spring Mrs MacLean and her lodger were going out together in his car on a Saturday, sometimes to a quiet tea-room on the outskirts of the city or further out into the country where they would stretch their legs for a bit before having a leisurely high tea in some small hotel where, as often as not, Mrs MacLean would inform waitress and sometimes waiters about Harry Veitch's egg allergy. Then Veitch would sit back and watch the dishes beckoned or waved away, would hear with an impassive face the detailed discussions of what had gone into the make-up of certain pies and rissoles, and would occasionally see Mrs MacLean reject a bare-faced egg outright. He never entered into such discussions. It almost seemed as though he had let her take over the entire poisonous side of his life. On the whole, he seemed to enjoy the dining-room dramas when all heads would turn and silence fall at the sound of Mrs

MacLean's voice rising above the rest; 'No, no, it's poison to him! Not at all – boiled, scrambled, poached – it's all the same. Poison!' But once in a while the merest shadow of irritation would cross his face, and on some evenings he drove home almost in silence, a petulant droop to his lips.

'But you did enjoy your supper, didn't you?'

'Quite.'

'And you didn't mind me saying that about the egg?'

'Why should I?'

'You see, I actually saw them through the door – whipping it up – even after I'd warned them. Even after I'd told them it was actual poison to you. They were whipping it up in a bowl – with a fork.'

'Exactly.'

'What do you mean – "exactly"?'

'I mean your description is obviously correct.'

'How stilted you make it sound. Why don't you relax – make yourself comfy?'

'While I'm driving? You want me to relax into this ditch for instance?' Very touchy he could be, almost disagreeable at times. But then he was allergic, wasn't he? A sensitive type.

Before long Mrs MacLean had given up eating eggs herself. She wouldn't actually say they disagreed with her nowadays. That would be carrying it too far. But how could what was poison to him be nourishment to her? She hardly noticed when the usual invitations to suppers with neighbours began to dwindle under her too vivid descriptions of eggs and their wicked ways. She was too busy devising new, eggless dishes for Veitch. By early summer she and her guest had explored the surrounding countryside and every out-of-the-way restaurant in the city. Mrs MacLean gave him a great deal. It was not only his stomach she tended. She gave him bit by bit, but steadily and systematically, the history of Edinburgh as they went about. 'You're standing on History!' she would exclaim, nudging him off a piece of paving-stone. Or, as he stood wedged momentarily in the archway of a close on a wild afternoon, her voice would rise triumphantly above the howlings and whistlings around him:

'You're breathing in History! Look at that inscription above your head!' He would step up cautiously onto slabs of wintry stone from which famous clerics had declaimed, sit in deep seats where queens had sat, while Mrs MacLean held forth herself. All the teaching experience of her younger days came back to her as she talked, and often when tourists were around a small crowd would gather and ask questions. One or two Americans might jot down her answers in notebooks and occasionally a photo was taken of her standing in the doorway of St Giles or with one elbow laid nonchalantly on the parapet of the Castle Esplanade. Sometimes Veitch got lost. He got lost for hours and hours, and after much searching Mrs MacLean would have to return home alone. It took a lot out of her. At times History really hurt.

By late autumn Veitch had got his job well in hand. It was expanding, he said. Really bursting its bounds. Mrs MacLean knew little about his job, but she identified with it and she was not one to stand in the way of his work. When he spoke of expansion and bursting bounds, however, refrigeration was the last thing she had in mind, but rather some mature and still seductive woman bursting through all the freezing restrictions into a boundless new life. But she felt a difference. He was not so available now. He worked late and had little appetite for the original eggless dishes she set before him at supper. Worst of all, when a few days of unexpected Indian Summer began, a sudden spate of work took him away from her for longer and longer sessions. He began to be busy on Saturday afternoons, and even on Sundays he found he must use the car to make certain contacts he'd had no time for during the week. Reluctantly, Mrs MacLean decided that until the pressure of work slackened she would simply take a few bus trips on her own while the weather lasted. She set off, good-naturedly enough, on solitary sprees at the weekends – as often as not ending up with tea alone in some country hotel or seaside café where they had been earlier in the year. She still had supper and breakfast talks with her lodger, but mostly it was herself talking to keep her spirits up. She never mentioned History now. Egg-talk was also out. In the bleak evenings she secretly yearned for the buttery omelettes and feathery soufflés she had whipped up in the old days.

One Saturday afternoon she took the bus right out into the country to an old farmhouse where they had been a couple of months ago. It stood well back from the road amongst low, gorse-covered hills, and winding through these were deep paths where you could walk for miles in a wide circle, eventually coming out again near the house. Mrs MacLean decided to take her walk after tea. There was nobody in the place but her spirits were rather higher than usual. She ate haddocks in egg sauce, pancakes, scones and plum jam and as she ate she talked on and off to the friendly girl who served it. She even managed to bring in a reference to a great friend of hers who was unable to eat egg in any shape or form, and for a while they discussed the peculiarities of people and their eating habits. Then she set off for her walk.

It was one of the last warm days of the year – so warm that after half an hour or so she had to remove her coat, and a mile further on uphill she was glad to lean on a gate and look down to where, far off, she could just see the line of the Crags and Arthur's Seat with the blue haze of the city beneath. Near at hand the weeds of the fields and ditches were a bright yellow, yet creamed here and there in the hollows with low swathes of ground-mist. But something jerked her from her trance. She realized with a shock that she was not the only person enjoying the surroundings. Unseen, yet close to her behind the hedge, there were human rustlings and murmurings. She bent further over the gate and craned her head sideways to look. Seated on a tartan rug which came from the back of her own drawing-room sofa was Harry Veitch, his arm round the waist of a young woman whose hair was yellow as egg yolk. Their legs lay together, the toes of their shoes pointed towards one another, and Mrs MacLean noted that under a dusting of seeds and straws Veitch's shoes still bore traces of the very shine she had put there the night before. For a few seconds longer she stood staring. From the distance of a field or two away it would have seemed to any onlooker that these three persons were peacefully enjoying the last moments of an idyllic afternoon together. Then, Mrs MacLean suddenly lifted her hands from the top of the gate as though it had been electrically wired, turned swiftly and silently down the way she had come and made for the bus route back to the city.

Sunday breakfast had always been a more prolonged affair than on other days, and the next morning Harry Veitch came downstairs late in green and white striped pyjamas under a maroon dressing-gown. He looked at ease, and on his forehead was a faint glow which was nothing more nor less than the beginning and end of a Scottish sunburn. For the weather had broken. Mrs MacLean greeted him, seated sideways at the table as usual to show that she had already eaten. But now Veitch was showing a strange hesitation in lowering himself into his seat. For some moments he seemed to find extraordinary difficulty in removing his gaze from the circumference of the plate before him, as though its rim were magnetic to the eyes which, try as they might to burst aside, were kept painfully riveted down dead on its centre. But at last, with tremendous effort, he managed to remove them. Casually, smiling, he looked round the room at curtains, pot-plant, firescreen, sideboard – greeting them first before he spoke. And when he spoke it was in an equable voice, polite and low-pitched.

'Mrs MacLean, I can't take egg. Sorry.'

'Can't take?' There was a cold surprise in her voice. Veitch allowed himself one darting glance at the smooth boiled egg on his plate and another at the mottled oval of his landlady's face, and again let his eyes roam easily about the room.

'No, it's an allergy,' he said.

Mrs MacLean now got up with the teapot in her hand and poured out a cup for her lodger. 'I don't quite catch your meaning, Mr Veitch,' she said, coming round and standing with the spout cocked at his ear as though she would pour the brown brew into his skull.

'An allergy, Mrs MacLean,' said Veitch, speaking with the distinct enunciation and glassy gaze of one practising his vocabulary in a foreign tongue. 'I have an allergy to egg.'

'Do you mean you want special treatment here, Mr Veitch?'

'Mrs MacLean, I am allergic to egg. Egg is poison to me. Deadly poison!'

Mrs MacLean's face was blank, her voice flat as she answered:

'Then why should you stay here? In an egg-house.'

'An egg-house!' The vision of a monstrous six-compartment eggbox had flashed before Veitch's eyes.

'Yes, I love eggs,' she replied simply. 'Eggs are my favourite. I shall order two dozen eggs tomorrow. There will be eggs, fresh eggs, for breakfast, for lunch, for supper. Did you know there are ways of drinking eggs? One can even break an egg into the soup for extra nourishment. I have books crammed with recipes specifically for the egg. There are a thousand and one ways . . . '

'Poison!' cried Harry Veitch on a fainter note.

'Yes, indeed . . . if you stay. A thousand and one ways . . . ' she agreed. And for a start – with the expression of an irate conjurer – she produced a second boiled egg out of a bowl and nimbly bowled it across the table towards her shrinking lodger.

The Stonethrower

Douglas Dunn

Even when he was a boy Stevenson could throw things further than anyone else. He noticed that when others threw stones they went about it with a jerky, nervous effort. By the time the stone had dropped to the earth they had just recovered the sense of what they were doing. Then, of course, they were too late to watch the stone soar, or hit the ground, or see the splash form and vanish on the pond.

With Stevenson it was different. He would spend minutes looking for a stone suitable to his hand, or the distance he intended it should go. He would get the feel of it, rubbing its surfaces with his fingers. He would look at it affectionately, almost as if it was a pet, and almost begin to feel sorry that he would have to lose it in the long grass of the fields, or the shallow pond blanketed with weed at the end of the quarry. Each throw was thought about and balanced. After a short run, a slight twist of his body, his arm whipped back and then jettisoned the stone with such quick strength that his body seemed to utter a crack.

The other boys were well used to his ritual. They watched with admiration, and had long ago stopped feeling that he overdid it. But while they kept their eyes on Stevenson he was watching the unfumbling path of the stone as it reached the limit of its climb and then fell in a clear line to the pond. A splash would form. The weed would be shocked into a small eruption and rise with a faint sound which a boy beside him would add to with his own 'Wurrooomph!' mimicking larger explosions. A boy with a gift for seeing things that weren't there might shout that he'd seen a frog jump, although to see that he would have needed a telescope. They were all willing to believe it. Once, at a shorter range, it had actually happened and everyone had seen it. It was remembered as The Day Stevenson Made the Frog Jump. It had leapt out of the broken weed and everyone had been delighted. It pleased Stevenson, too. But he didn't understand why they made such a fuss over it.

Stevenson was not inclined to throw at things. His targets were always unfeeling objects like ponds and fences, a cluster of berries at the top of a rowan tree, or in winter the black, unpopulated nests high in the rookery. The others often threw stones at birds as they sat on posts or hedges, but they were never accurate. Stevenson never did. He never threw at other boys either. He was quiet, his throwing was a personal thing, which he often did alone, coming back to the quarry after the rest had gone. It was an activity which engrossed him, although he could not understand why he liked it. It had happened. It was something he had made his own.

Once, however, he had thrown at someone. The quarry was on private ground. When they were just beginning to tire of the place for that day a man appeared waving a stick and shouting 'Clear off!' They jeered back, quickening their retreat at the same time. A few threw stones, but they were far short of their target. For them, the stone-throwing was a gesture, an impertinence. But they knew that if Stevenson threw it would be a different matter entirely. They egged him on. It was against his nature and he refused. But they persisted, someone put a stone in his hand. It was the right size for the distance, it had the feel of a stone he would have chosen for himself. So he took his usual short run, the boys held back a few paces ready to run away, the stone went high into the air, as it always did. The man was naturally surprised at the strength of the throw, but took his eyes off the stone and waved his stick at them. He could never have expected that a boy could have thrown so far. As the boys jogged backwards watching the man they saw the stone descend and land forcefully two or three feet in front of him. The man jumped a few inches and fell on his back. He had been startled and made to look silly. Delighted, making incredible yells and shouts, and proud of the great Stevenson, they ran off as he picked himself up. This was known as The Day Stevenson Made The Man Jump. It was one of the high spots of his reputation. It was much better than the day the frog had jumped.

It was something boys might remember when they were men.

Stevenson got no fun from that day. It was the quick muscular effort of the throw he liked, the sound the stone made as it left his hand and cut through the air near him, and then the silence of its climb and fall, and the harmless noise as it landed. He made larks of stone that climbed high and that sang only to his ears; he put pieces of the earth into flight in small parts. It wasn't skill, or cunning, or work. What it was he didn't know. But he *did* know that it was his.

As he grew older he threw more and more often, but now never in company, always alone. When he was taken on holiday he would stand on the beach throwing stones into the sea, searching over the shingle for perfect stones, round, smooth. He brought a bagful home with him and laid them in a straight line on the window-sill of his room. Sometimes he would take one or two from this larder of pebbles and take them to the quarry. Throwing them was his special pleasure. They reminded him of the beach and the sea. He reserved them for attempts on his record.

By the time he was fifteen he could throw right over the pond and over the edge of the cliff at the far end of the quarry. At school, they wanted him to bowl at cricket. He hated the sight of the batsman so close to him; he was too much of a human target. They made him putt the shot, but it seemed unnatural to Stevenson and he disappointed all those who had vaunted his legendary abilities. Throwing the cricket ball was a different matter entirely, but it is hardly a recognized event. Still, his friends were glad to see the great Stevenson's famous arm was as remarkable in action as they had remembered it.

When Stevenson was sixteen, his father moved to another town, and shortly after Stevenson and his mother went too. There was no quarry now. They lived near the centre of a large town and it took Stevenson twenty minutes on a bike to reach a place where it was safe to throw. Over a stretch of wasteland where slums had been cleared he grubbed among the pieces of stone and rubble for missiles that were the right size. It was dead earth. Houses, brick, concrete, had stifled it. Hardly a weed grew in it. Spiders and woodlice lived under his stones. It was not a good place. He had to wait for people to pass, for dogs to wander at their own speeds out of his line of fire. He was almost bored. Besides, he was beginning to think he should have outgrown this passion for stones and for throwing them. What fantasy did it enact? What state of being inside him did it try to describe? His body was taut and strong, he was getting bigger and heavier. Surely, he thought, it's time to give up throwing stones and take to throwing something else.

Birks, the games master at the new school, was always dressed in a tracksuit. He wore special athletic shoes and was always on the move. He pranced and trotted from one activity in the gymnasium to the other, he bounced along touch-lines being huffy and irritated. His voice was always loud and strident, pitched for shouting at butter-fingered relay teams, delinquent wingers, sleepy fly-halfs, timid batsmen. If a boy asked him for advice on throwing the discus or running the mile he looked at him as if to say, 'You'll never be good enough.' He picked his own athletes from the obviously endowed who caught his eye and then spent his time grooming them for the Inter-School Championships, urging, forcing, his efforts instilling them with fierce competitive drive. The other boys, 'the ruck' as he called them, were left to his indolent assistant master to put through drill, the old familiar exercises changing from one to another on the frantic blast of a whistle. 'Discus?' Birks said breathlessly in reply to Stevenson's question. 'No, you cannot. We've got Feirh and Huggett. I haven't time for another discus thrower.' And he sprinted away blowing his whistle in the direction of a group of boys lounging beside the long-jump pit.

Stevenson bought a discus in a sports shop, and a pamphlet on how to throw it. Each evening of the spring he practised in a public recreation field at the edge of the city. There was seldom anyone else there. Occasionally a runner would come in from the road and pad round the track three or four times to cool off, then disappear into the dressing-rooms; or some boys on bikes might race round the cinders for a few minutes. Stevenson knew nothing of weight training, or scientific methods of strengthening the muscles. His only training consisted of furious callisthenics for as long as he could keep going, and, of course, throwing itself.

On the school's sports day at the end of June he turned up with his discus. Birks was displeased. There were four other competitors, standing with Birks beside the circle. 'That's a senior discus,' Huggett said scornfully. 'How far can you throw *that*?' They all laughed. 'All right, Stevenson, you can throw your own,' Birks said, winking at the others. They suppressed their mirth in anticipation of Stevenson making a fool of himself.

Huggett threw first. His discus *was* smaller and lighter. It went far and was expertly thrown. Stevenson was impressed. 'Go on,' shouted Birks, 'You're next.' Stevenson went into the ring. From the very first Birks knew that Stevenson had somehow picked up more than the mere rudiments of the skill. He could tell by the way he stood, by the way he stepped into the circle. The look on his face was tense with interest. Huggett, too, was surprised, and watched closely. Neither of them knew of how stones had become a discus, how Stevenson's short run had become turns in the circle. He had transformed that primitive handling of stones into the sophisticated skill of a modern sport.

Birks followed the path of the discus with bewildered silence; Huggett swore. It landed far ahead of Huggett's mark. And it was the senior size and weight of discus. When it was measured the assistant master came running back to say it was 172 feet. Birks remembered that last week a member of the British team had thrown less. Nothing like this had ever happened in his career before. It frightened him. Stevenson was putting on flannels over his shorts. He didn't even have a tracksuit. Everyone was asking him questions.

Stevenson was asked to join an athletics club. Within weeks he was being visited by coaches well known in the sport. He threw in events in other cities, he went to London. Towards the end of the year he represented Great Britain in a match and won. He was then not yet eighteen. Coaches said there was really nothing they could teach him. There were a few crudities of style that could be smoothed over, that was all. The best mechanics of throwing he seemed to know already by intuition, discovered by feeling rather than following the advice of someone else; as if the identities of the famous Greek statues had entered his body. And there was something supremely natural and elemental in his disdain of competition that was far beyond the requirements of good sportsmanship.

All that would not have come as a surprise to the boys who had watched and admired him at the quarry. They had always known that it wasn't just a matter of muscle and skill. It was something better. A marvellous understanding of something he relished in his own body. A joy. A perfection. An enjoyment that came without study or the proximity of other people. And it did not surprise them that he had not outgrown that childish power. If they thought at all about Stevenson's gift they would have explained its nature by his humility. Hadn't he always refused to throw at a rabbit, or a crow on a fence, the old man in the quarry?

The humility wore away. By the time he was twenty Peter Stevenson was a household name. He was a veteran of international matches, the European champion, the holder of the British record, a man the British team could always rely on. Contest after contest, Stevenson gritted his teeth and made the discus fly to the limits of his strength. With each effort, each victory, the movements, the discus itself, the atmosphere of the stadium, all became alien to him. No matter how sporting or companionable the other competitors were, he detested them. His duty was to disappoint them. They took it in good grace; they even enjoyed it. They were friendly and did not hate him back, but looked forward to their own victories elsewhere, and one day their victories over Stevenson.

It was now the year of the Olympics. He was fussed over by coaches and officials, a rich well-known figure in the town made his private gymnasium available, his fame was an incentive for the city corporation to build new playing-fields, he received letters from schoolboys, offers of scholarships from American colleges. He trained, he practised. And then his arm began to feel strange and weak, as if a vital thread in it had withered; the distances he threw in training got shorter and shorter. Staleness harboured in his body like fat. He seemed ill. The coaches were alarmed. They took him to specialists. There was nothing wrong, they said.

Shortly before the season started with an unimportant event early in May, Stevenson disappeared. He went back to the town where he had lived as a boy and took a room in a hotel. He went back to the quarry. Seven years had passed since he had last thrown stones into its green pond. Now he was larger and stronger. The stones he had been used to seemed so small in his hands. Effortlessly, he could almost drop them into the pond; it was hardly a throw at all. It was ease itself to pitch the stones over the pond and into the broom and gorse on the uneven ground that stretched behind the cliff.

Each afternoon for a week he went back there. What had it meant to him, throwing, choosing the stone? It was something he had done and kept on doing. It was childish; it was absurd. And yet it was austere and magnificent, the sight of a stone racing through the air, the earth in flight. If he added up the weight of all he had thrown it would come to tons. It was foolish, a habit he should have put a finish to, an obsession he had stylized into a sport.

It was only when he realized that several times in the past days he had, almost without knowing it, thrown at the birds and hares that sometimes appeared in his line of fire, that what he had gone there to discover made itself known to him. He had betrayed an inner principle of his power. He was no longer gentle. His gift had been used for an assertion of himself over other people. It had made him famous. Competition was like throwing stones at birds and hares. It was a kind of attack, a firing. He must always win, must always disappoint other men. Poles, Americans, Russians, Frenchmen. He was tired of it. Why had he given in? The boys had admired his gift for its accuracy in striking others. They had made that fuss about the frog, about the old man who had been knocked on his back. Hardly a day had passed but they asked him to throw at a bird that perched itself in their way.

While he thought, a crow dropped itself on a post on the other side of the quarry. Could he hit it? If he had betrayed himself to the extent he was convinced he already had, he had better clinch it now and get used to the fact that the demands of others had changed his gift, had made it bad. It was no longer the pure thing it had been. He had sullied it with the manners of Birks and Huggett. It was now just something he could be good at.

With a powerful heave, a desperate, angry effort, the stone flew over the quarry. Struck, the crow rose from the post. Feathers separated and fell to the ground on the soft curves of the wind. The violence of it, and the silent aftermath of the feathers, and the empty space where the crow had stood, shocked him. He looked at the huge hand, the thick, strong wrist; it was a weapon at the end of his arm. A silent gun. An axe. He must see what he could do for the bird. Perhaps it could be tended, perhaps it was only stunned. He leapt over the rough ground, but the stones were loose. He felt the ground slide away from him. He fell over and grabbed, but everything was soft and wet with the Spring. There was nothing to catch hold of except stones and dirt, but the weight behind his grasping fingers tore him away from them. He went down towards the boulders at the edge of the pond.

He lay with his feet in the green weed, shaken but unhurt. Triangular heads of frogs popped and submerged again; wagtails glided to holes in the bank. Earth and stones from the bank he had disturbed still trickled down. He saw the crow fly away and was glad of it.

Then he looked up at the edge of the cliff where he had thrown from. So often, if someone had been able to sit here seven or more years ago, they would have seen him appear at that edge after his short run. As he looked a line of children appeared and stared down at him. They had been watching him from the scrub for the past few days. It seemed to Stevenson they were the boys of his own day come back in the guise of their younger selves to persuade him, to put stones in his hand, to point at finches exposed at the delicate, lithe end of a branch.

The children remembered this as The Day We Found

Stevenson in the Pond. They talked about it for a long time. For Stevenson pushed himself through the season and went to the Olympics. Much was hoped for. But he was far from his best. Nothing he could do would bring back the joy, nothing could retrieve it. His name's in the record book.

A Time to Dance

Bernard MacLaverty

Nelson, with a patch over one eye, stood looking idly into Mothercare's window. The sun was bright behind him and made a mirror out of the glass. He looked at his patch with distaste and felt it with his finger. The elastoplast was rough and dry and he disliked the feel of it. Bracing himself for the pain, he ripped it off and let a yell out of him. A woman looked down at him curiously to see why he had made the noise but by that time he had the patch in his pocket. He knew without looking that some of his eyebrow would be on it.

He had spent most of the morning in the Gardens avoiding distant uniforms but now that it was coming up to lunch-time he braved it on to the street. He had kept his patch on longer than usual because his mother had told him the night before that if he didn't wear it he would go 'stark, staring blind'.

Nelson was worried because he knew what it was like to be blind. The doctor at the eye clinic had given him a box of patches that would last for most of his lifetime. Opticludes. One day Nelson had worn two and tried to get to the end of the street and back. It was a terrible feeling. He had to hold his head back in case it bumped into anything and keep waving his hands in front of him backwards and forwards like windscreen wipers. He kept tramping on tin cans and heard them trundle emptily away. Broken glass crackled under his feet and he could not figure out how close to the wall he was. Several times he heard footsteps approaching, slowing down as if they were going to attack him in his helplessness, then walking away. One of the footsteps even laughed. Then he heard a voice he knew only too well.

'Jesus, Nelson, what are you up to this time?' It was his mother. She led him back to the house with her voice blaring in his ear.

She was always shouting. Last night, for instance, she had

started into him for watching TV from the side. She had dragged him round to the chair in front of it.

'That's the way the manufacturers make the sets. They put the picture on the front. But oh no, that's not good enough for our Nelson. He has to watch it from the side. Squint, my arse, you'll just go blind – stark, staring blind.'

Nelson then had turned his head and watched it from the front. She had never mentioned the blindness before. Up until now all she had said was 'If you don't wear them patches that eye of yours will turn in till it's looking at your brains. God knows, not that it'll have much to look at.'

His mother was Irish. That was why she had a name like Skelly. That was why she talked funny. But she was proud of the way she talked and nothing angered her more than to hear Nelson saying 'Ah ken' and 'What like is it?' She kept telling him that someday they were going back when she had enough ha'pence scraped together. 'Until then I'll not let them make a Scotchman out of you.' But Nelson talked the way he talked.

His mother had called him Nelson because she said she thought that his father had been a seafaring man. The day the boy was born she had read an article in the *Reader's Digest* about Nelson Rockefeller, one of the richest men in the world. It seemed only right to give the boy a good start. She thought it also had the advantage that it couldn't be shortened, but she was wrong. Most of the boys in the scheme called him Nelly Skelly.

He wondered if he should sneak back to the school for dinner then skive off again in the afternoon. They had good dinners at school – like a hotel, with choices. Chips and magic things like rhubarb crumble. There was one big dinner-woman who gave him extra every time she saw him. She told him he needed fattening. The only drawback to the whole system was that he was on free dinners. Other people in his class were given their dinner money and it was up to them whether they went without a dinner and bought Coke and sweets and stuff with the money. It was a choice Nelson didn't have, so he had to invent other things to get the money out of his mother. In Lent there was the Black Babies; library fines were worth the odd 10p although, as yet, he had not taken a book from the school library – and anyway they didn't have to pay fines, even if they were late; the Home Economics Department asked them to bring in money to buy their ingredients and Nelson would always add 20p to it.

'What the hell are they teaching you to cook – sides of beef?' his mother would yell. Outdoor pursuits required extra money. But even though they had ended after the second term Nelson went on asking for the 50p on a Friday – 'to go horse-riding'. His mother would never part with money without a speech of some sort.

'Horse riding? Horse riding! Jesus, I don't know what sort of a school I've sent you to. Is Princess Anne in your class or something? Holy God, horse riding.'

Outdoor pursuits was mostly walking round museums on wet days and, when it was dry, the occasional trip to Portobello beach to write on a flapping piece of foolscap the signs of pollution you could see. Nelson felt that the best outdoor pursuit of the lot was what he was doing now. Skiving. At least that way, you could do what you liked.

He groped into his pocket for the change out of his 50p and went into a shop. He bought a giant thing of bubble-gum and crammed it into his mouth. It was hard and dry at first and he couldn't answer the woman when she spoke to him.

'Whaaungh?'

'Pick the paper off the floor, son! Use the basket.'

He picked the paper up and screwed it into a ball. He aimed to miss the basket, just to spite her, but it went in. By the time he reached the bottom of the street the gum was chewy. He thrust his tongue into the middle of it and blew. A small disappointing bubble burst with a plip. It was not until the far end of Princes Street that he managed to blow big ones, pink and wobbling, that he could see at the end of his nose which burst well and had to be gathered in shreds from his chin.

Then suddenly the crowds of shoppers parted and he saw his mother. In the same instant she saw him. She was on him before he could even think of running. She grabbed him by the fur of his parka jacket and began screaming into his face.

'In the name of God Nelson what are you doing here? Why aren't you at school?' She began shaking him. 'Do you realize what this means? They'll put me in bloody jail. It'll be bloody Saughton for me, and no mistake.' She had her teeth gritted together and her mouth was slanting in her face. Then Nelson started to shout.

'Help! Help!' he yelled.

A woman with an enormous chest like a pigeon stopped. 'What's happening?' she said.

Nelson's mother turned on her. 'It's none of your bloody business.'

'I'm being kidnapped,' yelled Nelson.

'Young woman. Young woman . . . ' said the lady with the large chest trying to tap Nelson's mother on the shoulder with her umbrella, but Mrs Skelly turned with such a snarl that the woman edged away hesitatingly and looked over her shoulder and tut-tutted just loudly enough for the passing crowd to hear her.

'Help! I'm being kidnapped,' screamed Nelson, but everybody walked past looking the other way. His mother squatted down in front of him, still holding on to his jacket. She lowered her voice and tried to make it sound reasonable.

'Look Nelson, love. Listen. If you're skiving school do you realize what'll happen to me? In Primary the Children's Panel threatened to send me to court. You're only at that Secondary and already that Sub-Attendance Committee thing wanted to fine me. Jesus if you're caught again. . . . '

Nelson stopped struggling. The change in her tone had quietened him down. She straightened up and looked wildly about her, wondering what to do.

'You've got to go straight back to school, do you hear me?'

'Yes.'

'Promise me you'll go.' The boy looked down at the ground. 'Promise?' The boy made no answer.

'I'll kill you if you don't go back. I'd take you myself only I've my work to go to. I'm late as it is.'

Again she looked around as if she would see someone who

would suddenly help her. Still she held on to his jacket. She was biting her lip.

'O God, Nelson.'

The boy blew a flesh-pink bubble and snapped it between his teeth. She shook him.

'That bloody bubble gum.'

There was a loud explosion as the one o'clock gun went off. They both leapt.

'O Jesus, that gun puts the heart sideways in me everytime it goes off. Come on son, you'll have to come with me. I'm late. I don't know what they'll say when they see you but I'm bloody taking you to school by the ear. You hear me?'

She began rushing along the street, Nelson's sleeve in one hand, her carrier bag in the other. The boy had to run to keep from being dragged.

'Don't you dare try a trick like that again. Kidnapped, my arse. Nelson if I knew somebody who would kidnap you – I'd pay *him* the money. Embarrassing me on the street like that.'

They turned off the main road and went into a hallway and up carpeted stairs which had full-length mirrors along one side. Nelson stopped to make faces at himself but his mother chugged at his arm. At the head of the stairs stood a fat man in his shirtsleeves.

'What the hell is this?' he said. 'You're late, and what the hell is that?' He looked down from over his stomach at Nelson.

'I'll explain later,' she said. 'I'll let him stay in the room.'

'You should be on *now*,' he said and turned and walked away through the swing doors. They followed him and Nelson saw, before his mother pushed him into the room, that it was a bar, plush and carpeted with crowds of men standing drinking.

'You sit here Nelson until I'm finished and then I'm taking you back to that school. You'll get nowhere if you don't do your lessons. I have to get changed now.'

She set her carrier bag on the floor and kicked off her shoes. Nelson sat down watching her. She stopped and looked over her shoulder at him, biting her lip.

'Where's that bloody eyepatch you should be wearing?'

Nelson indicated his pocket.

'Well wear it then.' Nelson took the crumpled patch from his pocket, tugging bits of it unstuck to get it flat before he stuck it over his bad eye. His mother took out her handbag and began rooting about at the bottom of it. Nelson heard the rattle of her bottles of scent and tubes of lipstick.

'Ah,' she said and produced another eyepatch, flicking it clean. 'Put another one on till I get changed. I don't want you noseying at me.' She came to him pulling away the white backing to the patch and stuck it over his remaining eye. He imagined that the tip of her tongue was stuck out, concentrating. When she spooned medicine into him *she* opened her mouth as well. She pressured his eyebrows with her thumbs, making sure that the patches were stuck.

'Now don't move or you'll bump into something.'

Nelson heard the slither of her clothes and her small grunts as she hurriedly got changed. Then he heard her rustle in her bag, the soft pop and rattle as she opened her capsules. Her 'tantalizers' she called them, small black and red torpedoes. Then he heard her voice.

'Just you stay like that till I come back. That way you'll come to no harm. You hear me Nelson? If I come back in here and you have those things off, I'll *kill* you. I'll not be long.'

Nelson nodded from his darkness.

'The door will be locked so there's no running away.'

'Ah ken.'

Suddenly his darkness exploded with lights as he felt her bony hand strike his ear.

'You don't ken things, Nelson. You *know* them.'

He heard her go out and the key turn in the lock. His ear sang and he felt it was hot. He turned his face up to the ceiling. She had left the light on because he could see pinkish through the patches. He smelt the beer and stale smoke. Outside the room pop music had started up, very loudly. He heard the deep notes pound through to where he sat. He felt his ear with his hand and it *was* hot.

Making small aww sounds of excruciating pain, he slowly

detached both eye-patches from the bridge of his nose outwards. In case his mother should come back he did not take them off completely, but left them hinged to the sides of his eyes. When he turned to look around him they flapped like blinkers.

It wasn't really a room, more a broom cupboard. Crates were stacked against one wall; brushes and mops and buckets stood near a very low sink; on a row of coat-hooks hung some limp raincoats and stained white jackets; his mother's stuff hung on the last hook. The floor was covered with tramped flat cork tips. Nelson got up to look at what he was sitting on. It was a crate of empties. He went to the keyhole and looked out but all he could see was a patch of wallpaper opposite. Above the door was a narrow window. He looked up at it, his eye-patches falling back to touch his ears. He went over to the sink and had a drink of water from the low tap, sucking in noisily at the column of water as it splashed into the sink. He stopped and wiped his mouth. The water felt cold after the mint of the chewing-gum. He looked up at his mother's things, hanging on the hook; her tights and drawers were as she wore them but inside out and hanging knock-kneed on top of everything. In her bag he found her blonde wig and tried it on, smelling the perfume of it as he did so. At home he liked noseying in his mother's room; smelling all her bottles of make-up; seeing her spangled things. He had to stand on the crate to see himself but the mirror was all brown measles under its surface and the eye-patches ruined the effect. He sat down again and began pulling at his chewing gum, seeing how long he could make it stretch before it broke. Still the music pounded outside. It was so loud the vibrations tickled his feet. He sighed and looked up at the window again.

If his mother took him back to school he could see problems. For starting St John the Baptist's she had bought him a brand new Adidas bag for his books. Over five pounds it had cost her, she said. On his first real skive he had dumped the bag in the bin at the bottom of his stair, every morning for a week and travelled light into town. On the Friday he came home just in time to see the bin lorry driving away in a cloud of bluish smoke. He had told his mother that the bag had been stolen from the playground during break. She had threatened to phone the school about it but Nelson had hastily assured her that the whole matter was being investigated by none other than the Headmaster himself. This threat put the notion out of his head of asking her for the money to replace the books. At that point he had not decided on a figure. He could maybe try it again sometime when all the fuss had died down. But now it was all going to be stirred if his mother took him to school.

He pulled two crates to the door and climbed up but it was not high enough. He put a third one on top and gingerly straightened, balancing on its rim. On tip-toe he could see out. He couldn't see his mother anywhere. He saw a crowd of men standing in a semi-circle. Behind them were some very bright lights, red, yellow and blue. They all had pints in their hands which they didn't seem to be drinking. They were all watching something which Nelson couldn't see. Suddenly the music stopped and the men all began drinking and talking. Standing on tip-toe for so long Nelson's legs began to shake and he heard the bottles in the crate rattle. He rested for a moment. Then the music started again. He looked to see. The men now just stood looking. It was as if they were seeing a ghost. Then they all cheered louder than the music.

Nelson climbed down and put the crates away from the door so that his mother could get in. He closed his eye-patches over for a while but still she didn't come. He listened to another record, this time a slow one. He decided to travel blind to get another drink of water. As he did so the music changed to fast. He heard the men cheering again, then the rattle of the key in the lock. Nelson, his arms rotating in front of him, tried to make his way back to the crate. His mother's voice said,

'Don't you dare take those eye-patches off.' Her voice was panting. Then his hand hit up against her. It was her bare stomach, hot and damp with sweat. She guided him to sit down, breathing heavily through her nose.

'I'll just get changed and then you're for school right away, boy.' Nelson nodded. He heard her light a cigarette as she dressed. When she had finished she ripped off his right eye-patch.

'There now, we're ready to go,' she said, ignoring Nelson's anguished yells.

'That's the wrong eye,' he said.

'Oh shit,' said his mother and ripped off the other one, turned it upside down and stuck it over his right eye. The smoke from the cigarette in her mouth trickled up into her eye and she held it half shut. Nelson could see the bright points of sweat shining through her make-up. She still hadn't got her breath back fully yet. She smelt of drink.

On the way out the fat man with the rolled up sleeves held out two fivers and Nelson's mother put them into her purse.

'The boy – never again,' he said, looking down at Nelson.

They took the number twelve to St John the Baptist's. It was the worst possible time because, just as they were going in, the bell rang for the end of a period and suddenly the quad was full of pupils, all looking at Nelson and his mother. Some sixth-year boys wolf-whistled after her and others stopped to stare. Nelson felt a flush of pride that she was causing a stir. She was dressed in black satiny jeans, very tight, and her pink blouse was knotted, leaving her tanned midriff bare. They went into the office and a secretary came to the window.

'Yes?' she said, looking Mrs Skelly up and down.

'I'd like to see the Head,' she said.

'I'm afraid he's at a meeting. What is it about?'

'About him.' She waved her thumb over her shoulder at Nelson.

'What year is he?'

'What year are you, son?' His mother turned to him.

'First.'

'First Year. Oh then you'd best see Mr Mac Dermot, the First Year Housemaster.' The secretary directed them to Mr Mac Dermot's office. It was at the other side of the school and they had to walk what seemed miles of corridors before they found it. Mrs Skelly's stiletto heels clicked along the tiles.

'It's a wonder you don't get lost in here, son,' she said as she knocked on the Housemaster's door. Mr Mac Dermot opened it and invited them in. Nelson could see that he, too was looking at her, his eyes wide and his face smiley.

'What can I do for you?' he said when they were seated.

'It's him,' said Mrs Skelly. 'He's been skiving again. I caught him this morning.'

'I see,' said Mr Mac Dermot. He was very young to be a Housemaster. He had a black moustache which he began to stroke with the back of his hand. He paused for a long time. Then he said,

'Remind me of your name, son.'

' – Oh I'm sorry,' said Mrs Skelly. 'My name is Skelly and this is my boy Nelson.'

'Ah yes Skelly.' The Housemaster got up and produced a yellow file from the filing cabinet. 'You must forgive me but we haven't seen a great deal of Nelson lately.'

'Do you mind if I smoke?' asked Mrs Skelly.

'Not at all,' said the Housemaster, getting up to open the window.

'The trouble is, that the last time we were at that Sub-Attendance committee thing they said they would take court action if it happened again. And it has.'

'Well it may not come to that with the Attendance Sub-Committee. If we nip it in the bud. If Nelson makes an effort, isn't that right Nelson?' Nelson sat silent.

'Speak when the master's speaking to you,' yelled Mrs Skelly.

'Yes,' said Nelson, making it just barely audible.

'You're Irish too,' said Mrs Skelly to the Housemaster, smiling.

'That's right,' said Mr Mac Dermot. 'I thought your accent was familiar. Where do you come from?'

'My family came from just outside Derry. And you?'

'Oh that's funny. I'm just across the border from you. Donegal.' As they talked Nelson stared out the window. He had never heard his mother so polite. He could just see a corner of the playing fields and a class coming out with the Gym teacher. Nelson hated Gym more than anything. It was crap. He loathed the changing rooms, the getting stripped in front of others, the stupidity he felt when he missed the ball. The smoke from his mother's cigarette went in an arc towards the open window. Distantly he could hear the class shouting as they started a game of football.

'Nelson! Isn't that right?' said Mr Mac Dermot loudly.

'What?'

'That even when you are here you don't work hard enough.'

'Hmm,' said Nelson.

'You don't have to tell me,' said his mother. 'It's not just his eye that's lazy. If you ask me the whole bloody lot of him is. I've never seen him washing a dish in his life and he leaves everything at his backside.'

'Yes,' said the Housemaster. Again he stroked his moustache. 'What is required from Nelson is a change of attitude. Attitude, Nelson. You understand a word like attitude?'

'Yes.'

'He's just not interested in school, Mrs Skelly.'

'I've no room to talk, of course. I had to leave at fifteen,' she said rolling her eyes in Nelson's direction. 'You know what I mean? Otherwise I might have stayed on and got my exams.'

'I see,' said Mr Mac Dermot. 'Can we look forward to a change in attitude, Nelson?'

'Hm-hm.'

'Have you no friends in school?' asked the Housemaster.

'Naw.'

'And no interest. You see you can't be interested in any subject unless you do some work at it. Work pays dividends with interest . . . ' he paused and looked at Mrs Skelly. She was inhaling her cigarette. He went on, 'Have you considered the possibility that Nelson may be suffering from school phobia?'

'Mrs Skelly looked at him. 'Phobia, my arse,' she said. 'He just doesn't like school.'

'I see. Does he do any work at home then?'

'Not since he had his bag with all his books in it stolen.'

'Stolen?'

Nelson leaned forward in his chair and said loudly and clearly,

'I'm going to try to be better from now on. I am. I am going to try, sir.'

'That's more like it,' said the Housemaster, also edging forward.

'I am not going to skive. I am going to try. Sir, I'm going to do my best.'

'Good boy. I think Mrs Skelly if I have a word with the right people and convey to them what we have spoken about, I think there will be no court action. Leave it with me, will you? And I'll see what I can do. Of course it all depends on Nelson. If he is as good as his word. One more truancy and I'll be forced to report it. And he must realize that he has three full years of school to do before he leaves us. You must be aware of my position in this matter. You understand what I'm saying, Nelson?'

'Ah ken,' he said. 'I know.'

'You go off to your class now. I have some more things to say to your mother.'

Nelson rose to his feet and shuffled towards the door. He stopped.

'Where do I go, sir?'

'Have you not got your time-table?'

'No sir. Lost it.'

The Housemaster, tut-tutting, dipped into another file, read a card and told him that he should be at R.K. in Room 72. As he left Nelson noticed that his mother had put her knee up against the Housemaster's desk and was swaying back in her chair, as she took out another cigarette.

'Bye love,' she said.

When he went into Room 72 there was a noise of oo's and ahh's from the others in the class. He said to the teacher that he had been seeing Mr Mac Dermot. She gave him a Bible and told him to sit down. He didn't know her name. He had her for English as well as R.K. She was always rabbiting on about poetry.

'You boy, that just came in. For your benefit we are talking and reading about organization. Page 667. About how we should divide our lives up with work and prayer. How we should put each part of the day to use, and each part of the year. This is one of the most beautiful passages in the whole of the Bible. Listen to its rhythms as I read.' She lightly drummed her closed fist on the desk in front of her.

' "There is an appointed time for everything, and a time for every affair under the heavens. A time to be born and a time to die; a time to plant and a time to uproot. . . . " '

'What page did you say Miss?' asked Nelson.

'Six-six-seven,' she snapped and read on, her voice trembling. ' "A time to kill and a time to heal; a time to wear down and a time to build. A time to weep and a time to laugh; a time to mourn and a time to dance. . . . " '

Nelson looked out of the window, at the tiny white H of the goalposts in the distance. He took his chewing gum out and stuck it under the desk. The muscles of his jaw ached from chewing the now flavourless mass. He looked down at page 667 with its microscopic print, then put his face close to it. He tore off his eye-patch thinking that if he was going to become blind then the sooner it happened the better.

The Yellow on the Broom

Betsy Whyte

'What's that you're doing, lassie?'

My mother's voice startled me as I was sitting in the tent combing my hair – when I should have been away to work. The others had left over half an hour earlier.

Then I heard Mary's voice answer Mother, 'I'm just washing out some clothes.' 'I can see that you're washing but, lassie dear, you can't hang your knickers out like that there with all the men passing by looking at them. Look, lassie, double them over like this or pin that apron over them and they will dry just as quickly. If Johnnie comes home and sees your knickers hanging there, he will be your death.'

Mother came back into the tent muttering to herself, 'God knows what he was doing marrying a scaldie for anyway. You can put sense into them no way.' Then she spoke to me. 'Are you not going to any work today?' 'I'm just going, Ma.'

When I stepped out of the tent, I met Mary. She had not argued back with Mother but had done as Mother told her. 'Are you going to the field?' she asked. 'Aye,' I answered. 'Are you?'

As the two of us made our way down the old road she asked me, 'Did you hear your mother at me again this morning?' 'Mother is only telling you for your own good. Remember the beating you got from Johnnie when you sat in front of the men with your legs apart?' (Traveller men hate their wives doing things like that. A traveller woman would never do so, anyway.)

Mary was not a traveller. Johnnie, my mother's nephew, had met her when he was working in Perth. She had worked in Stanley Mill and went into Perth some weekends, for her mother lived there. She had been cooped in the mill for five years and the fresh air and outside life since she married Johnnie had agreed with her. But she was a bit befuddled with some of our strange customs.

'Ach, you'll soon learn,' I told her. 'You've only been married four months.' We were all really fond of Mary.

Soon we reached the field where several men and women were pulling turnips. My father, uncles and their wives, Johnnie (Mary's man) and also a man called Hendry Reid who none of us was very fond of. Hendry was too soulless-hearted, having been known to kick and batter his wife and children – and horse when he had one.

This Henry Reid was talking away as they worked. 'That man is always ganshin',' I said to Mary. 'Some of the men are sure to lose the head with him one of these days. He is always bragging about how he can get other men's wives, and about what he done in the War, but my mother says that he hid himself in a cave in Argyllshire all the time of the War. His poor mother was trauchled to death carrying food for miles to him. Oh aye, he was a brave soldier!'

We picked up our hukes (sickles, if you like) and started to pull the neeps. Mary was not very good at it, but Johnnie helped her to keep up. Soon it was after midday and, although it was October, the sun was beaking down on us. Hendry was still ganshin'. My father and the other men and women could have seen him in hell. Nothing could have been more nerve-racking than his loud, squeaky, incessant voice.

Then Dad shouted to Mary and me. 'You two lassies go down to that farm and see if you can get a drop of milk, and if you see the old keeper ask him for a seed of tobacco for me. I'll have the water boiling for you coming back, so hurry up! Johnnie, you go for sticks – and Liza, you can look for some clean water.' (Liza was Mother's brother's wife.)

It was more than a mile to the farm, so Mary and I walked quickly down the old road. 'I could do with a smoke,' Mary said. 'Aye, and me too,' I answered.

Then Mary looked startled. 'Look over in that field. What are all they men doing over there?' 'That's shooters,' I told her. 'Do you not see their guns? They are just stopped for a smoke.' 'Smoke!' I said again. 'What's about asking them for tobacco?'

'I'm game if you are,' Mary said. So we climbed through the paling and walked across the field. 'They can only say aye or no,' I told Mary.

There must have been about twenty men with plus-fours, deerstalker hats and leather boots. As we drew near they stared at us. 'What are you doing here, and what do you want?' a huge man with a red mouser, and a face to match, shouted. He was holding a whisky flask in his hand, as were several of the others.

'I wonder if any of you would have a wee bit tobacco to spare?' I asked. 'It's for my father.' I thought Beetroot Face was going to have a fit. 'Get out of here before I put the dogs on you!' The other men were all laughing. But one of them said, 'Wait a minute. Give this to your father,' and he threw a tin which landed at my feet. 'Just take the tin with you,' he said. I lifted it and took to my heels, Mary after me. We threw ourselves over the fence and collapsed breathless and giggling, at the side of the old road.

'He is a civil man, that one with the face like a harvest moon,' I said. 'You wouldn't want for your supper if everybody was like him.' Mary looked blankly at me and said 'Eh?' I sometimes forgot that she wasn't a traveller, and didn't understand this travellers' habit of saying the opposite of what they meant.

'Never mind,' I said to her, opening the tin of tobacco. 'This is not tobacco, it's shag,' I said. 'Let me see.' Mary took the tin. 'It *is* tobacco. The very best of tobacco.' Well, I've never seen tobacco like that,' I answered her, 'but I'm going to make a fag with some of it anyway. Do you have a match?' 'No,' she said. 'Then we are as well worried as hung. We have tobacco now and no match. We'll get one down at the farm.'

'But wheesht, Mary! I hear something coming up the road. Come through the paling into the field and let it pass. It's a car of some kind.' It was a shooting brake. 'Sit down Mary, and they won't see us. Some of they gentry,' I said, as it passed along the narrow road. 'Come on and we'll hurry to the farm for milk.'

The back door of the farm was wide open and the savour of cooking and baking nearly took the heart from me. I hadn't as yet broken my fast. The farm-wife was a pleasant person. When we told her our errand she said, 'Aye, plenty, lassies – but it's been skimmed. Give me your flagon and I'll fill it for you.'

'Did you come down the way?' she asked, as she ladled the milk into the can. 'Aye,' I answered. 'Then you must have seen the Duchess passing, in a shooting brake, and her two bonny wee lassies with her. The Duke is up there somewhere with the shooters. They say he is a good shot. He's the Duke of York, you know, and he's married to Elizabeth, one of the Bowes-Lyons from Glamis Castle. His father is the King,' she went on.

'Do you mean that one of they men shooting up the road is the King's son?' I asked. 'That's what I'm telling you,' she answered. Mary and I exchanged glances. 'Shaness, shaness,' I whispered. The farm-wife was very pleased and excited at having seen the gentry. 'The Duchess is likely away up with their lunch,' she said. 'My two laddies are away beating for them.'

'Would you like a piece?' she asked. She came out with two large pieces of still-warm scone. 'Oh! Thank you very much, Missis.' Mary rived into her piece but me, being a traveller, thought about my daddy pulling heavy swedes and without even a smoke. The scone would have choked me if I had eaten it past him. 'If you don't mind, Missis, I'll take my piece up to my father. He is working just up the road a bit.' 'Och, just you eat it up, lass. I have plenty and I'll give you some to take away with you.' I sank my teeth into the scone. It was dripping with syrup and never, I thought, had I tasted anything better. 'Well, goodbye Missis, and thank you kindly for being so nice to us. God bless you.' 'Away you go, lassies, it's nothing.'

'I'm not going up the road,' I said to Mary. 'Come on and we'll cut across the fields.' As we hurried over the fields Mary said, 'You forgot to ask for a match.' 'Oh, so I did,' I answered. 'I'm that worried about begging that tobacco. Don't tell my daddy, mind.'

As we approached, Father asked sarcastically 'Where did you go for the milk, to Kirriemuir? I'm sure I could have been in Inverness the time you've taken.'

Instead of answering him I took the tin of tobacco out of my pocket, opened it and held it out to him. 'Where did you get that, lassie?' 'Lying on the ground,' I said truthfully. 'Look, boys!' Daddy turned to let them all see it.

Oh, barry! They were so pleased. Few of them had seen tobacco like this before. 'That's the kind of tobacco the gentry smoke,' Father explained to them. 'One of them must have lost it. Maybe one of those who are shooting over there.' (They had heard the gunshots from where we worked.) Soon they were all stuffing it into their pipes. Everyone had a clay pipe of his or her own. Yes, men and women.

'Give Mary a wee puckle to make a fag, Daddy.' 'Better Mary would learn to smoke the pipe. They fags are not good for anyone,' he said – passing Mary enough for a couple of roll-ups.

After a few minutes I asked Daddy for a draw of his pipe. 'Just a wee draw, Daddy, to taste it.' He took the pipe out of his mouth, wiped the shank with a corner of his shirt and handed it to me. This although I was only eleven years old at the time. Travellers are very fond of tobacco.

'Come, wee woman, I think that should do you now.' 'If you filled a kettle with tobacco this lassie would smoke it to the bottom through the stroup, without a halt,' he said to the others. 'I always put my pipe and matches into my bonnet at the front of the bed at night, and I've seen her when she thought her mother and I were sleeping. She would creep cannyways over our feet and get the pipe and matches to light it, then put them back canny again after she had her wee draw. When she was only four years old!'

'Now if a body had a drop tea . . . . ,' Uncle Duncan said. 'Who's making the tea?' The tea had been forgotten in the excitement over the tobacco.

Activities

Blood

Background notes

Keith Aitchison was born in Paisley in 1947, and is a civil servant. Another story by him, *The Seventh Man*, is published in *Scottish Short Stories 1982* (Collins 1982).

Pair work

1 This story has a strong dramatic quality, and unfolds like a film sequence. Discuss and note down how the author creates this quality and makes it compelling. It may be helpful to first list the scenes that you think would make up the film sequence. Present your findings to the class.

2 At fifteen, Martin had lost his father. Now, at nineteen, he welcomes Uncle Tim as a sort of father substitute, or role model. Is this wise? What does it tell us about Martin at the beginning of this story?

   Who are your role models? How and why did you choose them?

   Think of adults you used to think were 'infallible' when you were younger. Do you still look for infallibility in your role models?

3 What does Martin's mother think of Uncle Tim?

4 Explore in pairs the significance of the story's title. Locate key points and themes in the story which link with the title and note them down for class discussion.

Group work

1 Martin learns that his grandfather 'fought and died for Ireland'. Why does this discovery momentarily turn Martin's world upside-down? Why did Martin's mother keep this family information from her son? Was she right to do so? Report your views back to the class after group discussion.

2 There is some sex stereotyping in this story. Try to locate this, and discuss its implications.

3 The story has two locations: Glasgow and Belfast. Compare and contrast the setting and atmosphere and associations of the two places.

Then discuss the effect of place on the story before presenting your group's views in class.

Written assignments

1 'Romantic Ireland's dead and gone', wrote the poet W. B. Yeats in his poem *September 1913*. Write about how it died for Martin O'Brien in this story.
2 Under the heading '*Blood*: A Personal Response', write about the overall effect this story has on you.
3 Write a letter from Timothy to his sister, apologizing for putting ideas in Martin's head. Use details from the story to help you.

Kreativ Riting

Background notes

Brian McCabe, born in 1951, writes poetry and radio drama as well as fiction. Another story dealing with a boy trying to cope with the alien demands of school is *Feathered Choristers*, in *Scottish Short Stories 1979* (Collins 1979).

Pair work

1 Analyse, in pairs, PK's approach and attitude to his students. Is it familiar? Is it working? If not, why not?
  Might you say Joe's classroom has a hidden agenda? What is it? Prepare some notes for wider class discussion.
2 The story is written in colloquial Scots. Is Scots an effective language for this story? Make a list of the things Scots seems to be good and bad at in the story. Report your findings back to the class for general discussion.
3 Compare this story with *A Time to Dance* (page 114). How do you think Nelson Skelly would get on with Joe Murdoch? How would Nelson fit in to this class? Use details from both stories to support your views.

Group work

1 What do you think of PK's double period creative writing lesson for 4F? Has he planned it well? How would your group organize a good

creative writing activity for this class? Take notes and present them to the class as a model lesson plan.

2 Joe's piece 'MY OWN SELF AS OTHERS SEE ME' is quite good. Although he has chosen to print it (why?), it is succinct, grammatical and correctly spelt, and the punctuation is quite clever. What does this tell us about Joe?

Discuss Joe's character as it emerges in the story. Discuss his self-image, and how this affects his performance in class.

Written assignments

1 Write a review of this story for your own school paper. Among other things, refer to the story's idiom, to its authenticity (or otherwise), and to the culture of these boys and this classroom.

2 Discuss in pairs the best or worst class lesson you have had this term. Then write a short description of the lesson listing what was good or bad about it. Conclude with a summary of your own views of the lesson.

Exile

Background notes

Robin Jenkins, born in 1912, in Lanarkshire, has published about twenty novels – the best-known being *The Conegatherers* (1955), *Dust on the Paw* (1961) and *Fergus Lamont* (1979). He has also published a book of long short stories, *A Far Cry from Bowmore* (1973), which describes expatriate life on the Indian subcontinent. Jenkins taught English overseas for many years, in Afghanistan, Spain and North Borneo. *Exile*, written in the 1970s, is almost certainly rooted in personal experience and observation.

Pair work

Discuss in pairs how you reacted to this story by reference to the following questions. Note down your views for class discussion

1 Do you think Miss Struthers was wise to retire to Spain?

2 What kind of teacher do you think she had been? Pick out details from the story to support your views.

3 Do you find this story moving? Can you say why, or why not?

How does the style of the story help to create a sense of poignancy?

Group work

1   Discuss the proposition that 'distance lends enchantment to the view' in connection with this story. Do you agree that this would be a suitable subtitle for the story? Why, or why not?
   Think of one or two alternative subtitles for the story. Present them in class, and vote on the best.
2   How skillfully has Robin Jenkins shown us the character of Miss Struthers? Has he told us enough about her? Can you see her as a real person? Present your group's views to the class.
3   Script and role play the conversation between Mr Leitch, the gardener, and Miss Struthers on the pros and cons of retiring to Spain.

Written assignments

1   Miss Struthers has kept a diary since her retirement. Write up a week of her diary, sticking as faithfully as you can to her character in the story and using evidence from the text.
2   Write the letter from Miss Struthers to Margaret Lennox inviting her to spend her Easter holidays in Javea. Remember that 'in her invitation she had tried hard not to be begging for an acceptance'.
3   Write a short essay entitled 'Teachers are Human Beings Too'. Provide some evidence from your own experience, humorous or serious, to back up your claim.

The Star

Background notes

Alasdair Gray, born in 1934, in Glasgow, is a writer and illustrator. He trained at the Glasgow art school, and his interests in book design as well as in writing have coalesced in several of his own publications, with their highly distinctive covers, endpapers, artwork and typography. Gray's first novel was *Lanark*, published in 1981 to huge critical acclaim, since when he has become something of a cult figure.

Pair work

Discuss the following questions in pairs. Note down your views for later presentation in class.
1   This is a very short story from the author's collection entitled

Unlikely Stories Mostly (1982). Would you call *The Star* an unlikely story? Why, or why not? Is it any the worse for being an unlikely story?

2   Compare the classroom and the teacher in *The Star* with the classroom and the teacher in *Kreativ Riting* (page 18). Both stories seem to be about ways of coping with classroom conditions that seem difficult. Which of these stories do you prefer, and why?

Group work

1   As a group, discuss what in your opinion constitutes a story. What elements must a story have? Appoint group note-takers to list your views.

By your own definition, is *The Star* a story? Is it a good one? Report your views, with reasons, to the class.

2   Continuing on from the previous question, discuss what you think is the purpose of this story. Report your views to the class.

3   Find out something about surrealism. Who were some of the leaders and practitioners of this movement and what period do they date from? What were some of their artistic aims and objectives?

Can Gray's writing be better understood in the context of surrealism? What is your group's feeling about surrealist art and writing? Discuss your findings and your views with the class.

Written assignments

1   This story is so short it begs for a short sequel. Imagine the star becomes a sort of invisible friend – or comfort – for the boy in the story. Try to match Gray's style and write the sequel to *The Star*.

2   Write a short surrealistic story in the style of Alasdair Gray about an episode from your own life. Make the commonplace, real world collide with something extraordinary or surreal in order to convey the idea of incongruity and of the transformation that results.

Tutti Frutti

Background notes

Christopher Rush, born in 1944, was born and raised in St Monans, a small and picturesque East Fife fishing village where many of his stories are set. He is now a teacher of English in Edinburgh. As well as stories, Christopher Rush has also written poetry and produced filmscripts. His script for *Venus Peter* – also about growing up in a small fishing community – captures something of the atmosphere of *Tutti Frutti*.

Pair work

1   The story is a fictional and poetic treatment of the large subjects of first love and of tragic death. Make a list of the story's poetic features for presentation to the class.
2   Discuss how the writer deals with the subject of Mr Cargill's death. How does the narrator react? How does the dead man's daughter react?
3   There are five sections to the story, marked off with spaces – rather like a five act play. Discuss the structure of the story, and the 'pace' of the narrative. You might like to chart out the five sections to show key points where the pace of the story either slows or quickens.

Group work

1   Consider all the songs and poems and quotations with which this story is interspersed. Discuss the function of these elements in the story, and their effect on it. Report your views to the class. (You may wish to suggest a few alternative or additional effects.)
2   What is the effect of the ending of this story, and what do we infer from it?
3   Critics compare the work of Christopher Rush and George Mackay Brown. Compare *Tutti Frutti* with *The Tree and the Harp* (page 54), discussing and noting similarities and differences between the style of these stories. Appoint a group spokesperson to present your findings to the class.

Written assignments

1   Drawing out the tragedy, the comedy and the lyricism of this story, write your own critical review of the story for a local, East Fife newspaper.
2   Discuss in pairs exactly what is meant by the term 'lyrical'. Then write a short, lyrical story about an episode from your own first year at secondary school. Try working some poetry or snippets of popular songs of the day into your story.
3   In character, write a letter from the narrator of *Tutti Frutti* to Mr Leslie, his old English teacher. Imagine the narrator is now a second-year student at St Andrews University. Try to suggest some of the

things the narrator has learned about life now he is three years older and no longer lives at home.

The Tree and the Harp

Background notes

George Mackay Brown, born in 1921, at Stromness, in Orkney, is a poet, novelist and short story writer. He has lived at Stromness for most of his life, and most of his short stories are firmly based on Orkney community life. Mr Brown has published half a dozen collections of short stories, including *The Masked Fisherman* (1989), from which *The Tree and the Harp* is taken.

Pair work

In pairs, role play an interview between a reporter from the *Orkney Times* and Sophie Birsay after the reading of Mrs Maida's will. Then write notes for an article for the newspaper disclosing Sophie's news. Give the article an appropriate headline.

Group work

1　Discuss the role of the supernatural in this story. Do you feel it is handled successfully? Give reasons for your views and use details from the story as evidence to support them.

2　A reviewer has described *The Tree and the Harp* as 'a superior ghost story'. Why do you think the word superior has been used? Can you describe the story better – and a little more fully?

Present your group's description of the story to the rest of the class. Select the best group description (other than your own), giving reasons for your choice.

3　Although the Hall, where Sophie lives, was still without electricity, this is a story of one of the smaller islands of Orkney from not so long ago – perhaps from the 1970s. Discuss in groups the advantages and disadvantages of contemporary life in small, isolated, island communities. Refer to Sophie's experiences. You might like to compare this way of life with that depicted in *Remember Me* (page 82).

Written assignments

1 Write an obituary notice for Mrs Maida to appear in the *Orkney Times*. Include as much factual information about her life as you can find from the story (her background, character, etc).

2 Write an account of a ghostly experience in your own life. Make it scary if you can. You could write either from your own point of view, or from that of someone who shared the experience with you.

Her Brother Died

Background notes

George Friel (1910–1975) was a Glaswegian schoolmaster and is best remembered nowadays for his novels *The Boy Who Wanted Peace* (1964) – which reviewers compared with *Lord of the Flies* – and *Mr.Alfred, M.A.* (1972), which was about a Glasgow schoolmaster. Like his novels, Friel's short stories are deeply rooted in his observation and experience of working-class Glasgow life.

Her Brother Died first appeared in 1936. An everyday fact of working class tenement life in the 1930s was a high mortality rate, with consumption (or tuberculosis) a common and often fatal illness right up to the 1950s. And perhaps the 'sorrowful weariness' of Mrs Ramsay might now be treated as ME.

Group work

1 Review the story in groups. Say why you like or dislike it, giving reasons for your views. What do you think of the ending, in particular? Present your group's views to the rest of the class.

2 Imagine that Mrs Hamilton is being grilled by the 'gossip hungry neighbours' in the tenement after the events in the end of the story. Try to script and role play the dialogue. The 'gossiping matrons' could be a sort of disapproving Greek chorus, commenting on the action as reported by Mrs Hamilton.

3 Use details from the story to describe the brother's death, and the arrangements for the funeral. How did the bereaved mother and sister cope? What happened after Mrs Hamilton went into the front room? What did she say? What did Mona Ramsay say and do? You may like to script this dialogue and present it to the rest of the class.

Written assignments

1   Imagine Mona Ramsay kept a diary. What sort of information do you think she would confide to it? Write her diary entries for the day her brother died, and for the day of the funeral.

2   *Her Brother Died* is in many ways a typical George Friel story: in its setting, its ironic tone and theme. Write a short review of it. Comment on how well it has survived the test of time.

Old Wives' Tales

Background notes

Wilma Murray, born in 1939, is from Aberdeenshire and lectures at Northern College of Education, Aberdeen. Her stories have appeared in various magazines and also been broadcast on radio.

Pair work

1   Like *Remember Me* (page 82), this story is a monologue which follows the 'stream of consciousness' approach to writing. The author gives the impression that all her thoughts are being written down, without much selection.

   Discuss how effective such a technique is as a way of telling this story. Who is the author actually talking to? Research and read other pieces – poems or novels – written in this form. How well do they work? Note down your own views for discussion in class.

2   Discuss the significance of *Humpty Dumpty* in this story. How important is this as a recurring theme, or *leitmotiv*, in the story?

3   We have already compared this story with *Remember Me*. Compare the importance of Fiona to the narrator of that story, with the unborn child in *Old Wives' Tales*.

4   How far does the author carry the parallels with the Christian Nativity – 'three wise men', 'one wise woman', etc? How significant is this parallel?

Group work

1   People sometimes think they know all they need to know about a subject because they have read 'the book'. The narrator of *Old Wives'*

Tales is perhaps such a person at the beginning of this story. Discuss in groups whether you can separate knowledge (or wisdom?) into two categories of:

   a) what you can learn from books, and

   b) what you can only learn from experience?

   Compare your lists with those of other class groups.

2   Examine the use of colloquial/informal English in this story. Is it appropriate here? Discuss the effect it has on the story.

3   What does the mother wish and/or fear for her unborn child? How does her list compare with the one you would make up for your child, if you had one?

Written assignments

1   Write a short, stream of consciousness monologue covering a particular event or recent experience in your own life. Decide beforehand exactly who you are addressing – your mother, your penpal in America, etc. It might be a good idea to write about your feelings after the event, rather than about the event itself.

2   Write a letter from the narrator of *Old Wives' Tales* to her grandmother after the birth of her baby.

Remember Me

Background notes

Naomi Mitchison, born in 1897, has published over 70 books, including novels, short stories, children's books, poetry, autobiography and diaries. She was an early member of CND, an Argyll county councillor, and a strong social conscience is evident in much of her work.

   You might consider comparing *Remember Me* with other visions of life after the holocaust, such as Edwin Muir's poem *The Horses*, or work by Nevil Shute (*On the Beach*, 1957), Raymond Briggs (*When The Wind Blows*, 1982) and Robert Swindells (*Brother in the Land*, 1984).

Pair work

Discuss the style of this story – the matter-of-fact reporting of events, which is neither dramatic, melodramatic nor apocalyptic. Much is implied, but not stated. Even after such terrible events, people struggle on with their lives. Select details from the story that exemplify this style.

How effective is all this? Note down your views for wider discussion in class.

Group work

1   This is an eerie and rather harrowing story. It describes how society starts to crumble and how essential services grind to a standstill after a nuclear explosion. 'It is queer how much we took for granted in the old days,' says the narrator, 'now we are back to something much older.'

What are the things the narrator missed most? Make a list. What are some of the 'older things' the community has gone back to? Make another list.

Discuss what you think the community's prospects are. Present your conclusions to the class.

2   In some respects, the narrator is lucky – she has Fiona and the Community Council to keep her going. But she feels that 'love has been killed in me'. What does the group think she means by this?

Written assignments

1   The agenda for Community Council meetings has changed considerably since the bomb dropped. Compile two probable agendas for a rural community council meeting – one for before the disaster and one for after, to show how priorities have changed.

2   It is 'just not enough to be brave' the narrator says. What do you think she means by this? Discuss this statement with a partner, and then explain it in writing in your own words.

3   Imagine yourself resident in a stricken and isolated community like the one described. Out of the blue, you suddenly receive radio contact from a radio ham in the far west of Ireland – after two years of total isolation. With a partner, role play and then script the dialogue between yourself and the radio ham. You may like to try recording the dialogue.

Allergy

Background notes

Elspeth Davie, born in Ayrshire, in 1919, has published four novels and four collections of short stories, winning the Katherine Mansfield Award for short stories in 1978. She is also an artist. Although much of her fiction has an Edinburgh setting, it is really as a creator of character that Elspeth Davie excels. Her work reminds us, as she says, that 'the strange, the desolating and the ludicrous is happening to us all the time' – for it combines the serious and the ridiculous as she sketches her vignettes of everyday life and human relationships.

Pair work

1   Is this a story in which you experience the desire to take sides? Whose side are you on, and why? List your reasons.
    Do you change sides during the course of the story?
2   Compare the abrupt ending of this story with that of *Her Brother Died* on page 76. How satisfactory do you find these endings?

Group work

1   There are some very understated, 'deadpan' touches in this story. Try to locate some of these and note them down. Then discuss as a group whether or not you find this a humorous story and present your views through a group spokesperson to the rest of the class.
2   Discuss the change in Mrs MacLean's attitude to Harry Veitch after she discovers him with another woman. Does the author handle this well? Are you convinced by this 'change'?

Written assignments

1   In pairs, discuss what might have happened next. Then write your sequel to the story, in your own style.
2   We seem to discover far more about Mrs MacLean in this story than we ever learn about Harry Veitch. Do you agree? Write a letter from Harry Veitch to his old mother in the south of England notifying her of his change of address and of his reasons for changing lodgings.
3   Write about the significance of the egg in this story. How and why is it important?

The Stonethrower

Background notes

Douglas Dunn, born in 1942, in Renfrewshire, is best known as a poet, especially after winning the prestigious Whitbread Award for *Elegies* (1985). He is also an occasional writer of short stories, and there is a published collection of these – *Secret Villages* (1985). Dunn was a librarian at the University of Hull for many years, where he was a colleague of the poet Philip Larkin. He now lives at Tayport, in Fife.

Pair work

1   Discuss how you feel the 'change' in Stevenson is managed by the author. Does he handle this aspect of the story successfully?
    Make notes plotting the stages of Stevenson's change.
2   Is this a cautionary tale – what not to do with natural talent? Discuss and note down your ideas on this for wider class discussion.
3   Look at the author's clear, detailed description of an apparently commonplace event – throwing a stone. The essential nature of the event is conveyed: 'unfumbling path', 'clear line', etc.
    See if you can do this, in pairs, about some other everyday event. Read your description to the class.

Group work

Think about the following questions arising from *The Stonethrower* and discuss them in your groups.
1   '(Stevenson) was no longer gentle . . . Competition was like throwing stones at birds . . . attack.' Would you say there was a moral to this story, such as 'live and let live' or do not be manipulated? Or something else?
    Is gentleness a fashionable virtue?
2   How do you feel about competitive sport? Does it bring out the best or the worst in people?
3   Is it possible nowadays to do things merely because you like doing them, without thought of benefit or profit? Do you admire people who like to do things for their own sake?
    Contrast public fame with private fulfilment. Can you think of any sports people or other celebrities who have found it difficult to reconcile these two things.

Written assignments

1   Script and role play an interview with Stevenson on TV prior to the Olympic Games. Draw up some searching questions to ask. Make sure your replies are in character with the Stevenson of the story.
2   Write a short review of this story.

A Time to Dance

Background notes

Bernard MacLaverty, born in 1942, in Belfast, grew up in Northern Ireland. He taught for a number of years in Edinburgh and on Islay, but now writes full time and lives in Glasgow. He has written for film, for radio and for TV, as well as fiction for children and adults.

Pair work

Discuss the following questions about the story, making notes as you go, so that you can then present your views to the class.
1   Who is narrating this story? Could you say the narrator had a point of view?
2   What can you say about the 'tone' of this story? Do you like it? Why or why not?
3   What hope is there for Nelson? What are his strengths and weaknesses? Is he likely to change his attitude?
4   Who has more to teach Nelson – his mother or the lady in room 72 who is 'always rabbiting on about poetry'?
5   What do you think of the teacher who speaks to Nelson and his mother? How is Nelson likely to be treated by staff at St John the Baptist Secondary (assuming Mr MacDermot is a typical member of staff)?

Group work

1   The *Spectator* review of his novel *Cal* said that MacLaverty 'describes the sad, straitened, passionate lives of his characters with tremendously moving skill'. Discuss the terms in which you would critically review this story. Take notes and present your group review to the class. Vote on the best review (other than your own).
2   Discuss how you feel about unusual first names for children. Think of a few that you like and dislike. List them. What conclusions can the group draw?
3   Explore the theme of social deprivation and its effects on educational performance. List ways in which Nelson is deprived using evidence from the story.

Written assignments

1   Mrs Skelly writes a letter to her mother in Belfast. In it, she talks

about Nelson's and her own problems. Write the letter. Include relevant details from the story. You will also need to decide how much Mrs Skelly will tell her mother about her own work.

2   Write a letter to Bernard MacLaverty asking him about aspects of the story which you did or didn't understand or like. Giving good critical reasons, tell him what you thought of the story.

The Yellow on the Broom

Background notes

Betsy Whyte, 1919–1988, was born at Blairgowrie into a family of travelling people. Her autobiography, *The Yellow on the Broom*, vividly describes a childhood spent, in summer, doing farmwork and odd jobs and travelling the open road and living in tents. The winters were spent cooped up in an old house pining for the first sign of spring – the yellow on the broom. Betsy Whyte's fund of stories and anecdotes link today's reader with an oral tradition which was once very powerful in Scottish literature.

You may like to compare this extract with a rather different story about traveller folk: it is called *A Matter of Behaviour*, by Naomi Mitchison (published in *A Girl Must Live*, 1990).

Pair work

1   Discuss the role of women in the travellers' society. What do you think about it?

2   What customs and standards of behaviour of the travellers are different from those of what is termed 'polite society'? Make a list.

Group work

1   Travellers have a special language or idiom called traveller cant. Travellers used their cant in a special way – they could seem to outsiders to be having a normal conversation while in reality giving all sorts of special messages to any traveller people listening. Traveller cant is now dying out quite rapidly.

As a group, you could devise your own classroom cant, or school cant, i.e. your own special vocabulary or idiom. Discuss the sort of contexts in which this could prove most useful. Then script a group conversation to perform before the rest of the class, and see if they can guess what you are talking about.

Here is an example of a sporting idiom, or cant, which means very little to non-cricket enthusiasts:

> Welcome to our overseas listeners. This is John Arlott from Lords, where Lillee has just bowled another maiden over, and England are on 358 for 2. Snow – the night-watchman – went for a duck, he tried to drive Gilmour for 6 and got an edge to the outswinger. Then Edrich was leg before to Thomson. Chappell running up to bowl his left arm off-spinners – no, its the Chinaman. Steele hooks him smartly past square leg – third man running round but he can't stop the boundary. Some field changes now – third slip to deep fine leg, point to extra cover, mid-on to silly mid-off. Lovely shot there – late cut behind deep point . . .

2   One of the great wonders of the oral tradition in literature was how it managed to survive without being written down. Try in groups to devise a simple five minute story for narration to a wider audience. Then let each member of the group record the story separately. Finally, play the different versions of the story back to the group. Are there any significant differences? Do the recordings tell you anything about the oral tradition?

3   *The Yellow on the Broom* was a bestseller on publication. Discuss why this should have been so, and present your group's conclusions to the rest of the class.

4   The episode described in the passage probably dates to the early 1930s. Do you think there are still traveller folk today? What do you know about today's travellers? What kind of life do you think they have now? Present your group's views to the class.

Written assignment

One reviewer described *The Yellow on the Broom* as 'curiously happy, bright and tolerant'. Write your own book review of this excerpt, which is taken from the very beginning of Betsy Whyte's story.

Extended Activities

1   Any society is a society in conflict, and Scotland is no exception. And any anthology that does not reflect this truth is a lie.
        Do you agree? What are some of the main social conflicts depicted in this book?

2   What are the advantages/disadvantages of a 'national' anthology of this kind? Would you like to read an American or an Australian anthology, for example? Why or why not?

3   These are all Scottish stories. Is this a disadvantage when it comes to introducing them to readers in England, Europe, Australia or North America? List the stories that you think will travel well outside of Scotland, and make another list of those that will have less appeal beyond Scotland. What general conclusions can you draw?

4   What is the general effect of this set of stories? Are there any missing ingredients you'd like to have seen better covered in this collection?

5   Comment on the position and treatment of women in these stories, with particular reference to two of the following: *Tutti Frutti*, *The Tree and the Harp*, *Her Brother Died*, *Old Wives' Tales*, *Allergy*, *The Yellow on the Broom*.

6   What political themes come out of this anthology? Do the writers express their nationalism objectively, subjectively, explicitly or not at all?

7   'My kind of story, my kind of writer'. Write an appreciation of the story in this collection which most closely fits this description for you.

8   Compare and contrast the use of idiom and dialect in two stories. Comment on the effect and the effectiveness of the language and the use to which it is put in the stories.

9   Compare and contrast the narrators' viewpoint in three stories. What is their point of view in relation to the main characters? Are they themselves main characters in their stories?

10   Imagine you are to produce an illustrated version of this book. What sort of pictures would you commission? Drawings? Photos? A mixture? One artist or a variety of styles? Where would you position your illustrations? Write a short report or 'art brief' listing the kinds of illustration you would commission.

11   Write a review of this anthology, either for the *Glasgow Herald*, the London-based *Independent*, or the *New York Review of Books*.

12   Some of these stories would make good films. Which one would you choose to adapt for film or TV? Explain why you have selected the story, and in what ways you think it would make a good film. You could conclude the assignment with a plan showing the sequence of scenes and a page or two of sample script.

Wider Reading

This section offers a bibliography for possible further reading. You are particularly invited to read more work by those authors whose stories specially appealed to you in this collection.

Assignments

Here are one or two specific suggestions for work:
1   Build up a folio on one or two of the authors whose stories you have particularly enjoyed in this book. Find out as much as you can about them and their work. Trace their development as writers.
2   Research the work of one Scottish writer of short stories not included in this collection. Make sure you find someone whose work you like. You could write a critical piece on your chosen author or write comparing them with several of the writers who appear in this anthology.
3   Think about the criteria you would follow if you were compiling your own anthology of stories. Make notes of your proposed title, the themes you want to cover, the readership you are aiming at, etc. Then research your contents. Be prepared to explain and discuss your approach in class.

General anthologies

Gifford, Douglas (ed.), *Scottish Short Stories 1800–1900*, John Calder 1971

Hendry, J.F. (ed.), *The Penguin Book of Scottish Short Stories*, Penguin 1970

Jarvie, Gordon (ed.), *The Wild Ride and Other Scottish Stories*, Viking Kestrel 1986, Puffin 1987

MacDougall, Carl (ed.), *The Devil and the Giro: Two Centuries of Scottish Stories*, Canongate 1989

Murray, Ian (ed.), *The New Penguin Book of Scottish Short Stories*, Penguin 1983

Scottish Short Stories, Collins/Scottish Arts Council. Annual anthologies of stories published since 1973. Various editors.

Other books by writers in this collection

George Mackay Brown

A Calendar of Love, Hogarth 1967, Grafton 1988. Short stories.
A Time to Keep, Hogarth 1969. Short stories.
Greenvoe, Hogarth 1972, Penguin 1976. Novel.
Magnus, Hogarth 1973, Richard Drew 1988. Novel.
Hawkfall, Hogarth 1974, Granada 1983. Short stories.
Selected Poems, Hogarth 1977.
Andrina and Other Stories, Chatto 1983. Short stories.
The Masked Fisherman, John Murray 1989. Short stories.

Elspeth Davie

Providings, John Calder 1965. Novel.
The Spark, John Calder 1968. Short stories.
Creating a Scene, John Calder 1971. Novel.
The High Tide Talker, Hamish Hamilton 1976. Short stories.
Climbers on a Stair, Hamish Hamilton 1978. Novel.
The Night of the Funny Hats, Hamish Hamilton 1980. Short stories.
A Traveller's Room, Hamish Hamilton 1985. Short stories.
Coming to Light, Hamish Hamilton 1989. Novel.

Douglas Dunn

Secret Villages, Faber 1985. Short stories.
Elegies, Faber 1985. A poem sequence on the death of his wife.
Selected Poems 1964–1983, Faber 1986.

George Friel

The Boy Who Wanted Peace, John Calder 1964, Polygon 1985, Corgi 1987. Novel.
Grace and Miss Partridge, John Calder 1969. Novel.
Mr Alfred, M.A.., John Calder 1972, Canongate 1987. Novel.
A Friend of Humanity, ed. Gordon Jarvie, Polygon 1992. Short stories.

Alasdair Gray

Lanark: A Life in Four Books, Canongate 1981, Panther 1982. Novel.
Unlikely Stories Mostly, Canongate 1982, Penguin 1984. Short stories.
1982, Janine, Jonathan Cape 1984, Penguin 1985. Novel.

The Fall of Kelvin Walker, Canongate 1985, Penguin 1986. Novel.
Lean Tales (with James Kelman and Agnes Owens), Jonathan Cape 1985. Short stories.
Something Leather, Jonathan Cape. 1990, Novel.
McGrotty and Ludmilla, Dog and Bone 1990. Novel.

Robin Jenkins

The Conegatherers, Macdonald 1955, Penguin 1983. Novel.
The Changeling, Macdonald 1958, Canongate 1990. Novel.
Dust on the Paw, Macdonald 1961, Richard Drew 1986. Novel.
A Far Cry from Bowmore and Other Stories, Gollancz 1973. Short stories.
Fergus Lamont, Canongate 1979. Novel.

Brian McCabe

The Lipstick Circus, Mainstream 1985. Short stories.
One Atom to Another, Polygon 1987. Poetry.
The Other McCoy, Mainstream 1990. Short stories.

Bernard MacLaverty

Secrets and Other Stories, Blackstaff 1977. Short stories.
Lamb, Jonathan Cape 1980, Penguin 1981. Novel.
A Time to Dance and Other Stories, Jonathan Cape 1982, Penguin 1985. Short stories.
Cal, Jonathan Cape 1983, Penguin 1984. Novel.

Naomi Mitchison

The Corn King and the Spring Queen, Jonathan Cape 1931, Virago 1983. Novel.
The Bull Calves, Jonathan Cape 1947, Richard Drew 1985. Novel.
Five Men and a Swan, Allen and Unwin 1958. Short stories.
What Do You Think Yourself? Paul Harris 1982. Short stories.
Beyond This Limit, ed. Isobel Murray, Scottish Academic Press 1986. Short stories.
A Girl Must Live, ed. Isobel Murray, Richard Drew 1990. Short stories.

Christopher Rush

Peace Comes Dropping Slow, Ramsay Head 1983. Short stories.

A Resurrection of a Kind, Aberdeen University Press 1984. Poetry.
A Twelve-month and a Day, Aberdeen University Press 1985. Short
  stories.
Two Christmas Stories, Aberdeen University Press 1988. Short stories.
Into the Ebb, Aberdeen University Press 1989. Short stories.

Betsy Whyte

The Yellow on the Broom: the Early Days of a Traveller Woman, Chambers
  1979, Futura 1986. Memoirs, autobiography.
Red Rowans and Wild Honey, Canongate 1988. Sequel to *The Yellow on
  the Broom*.

Anthologies by some other Scottish short story writers

Neil Gunn, *The White Hour*, Faber 1950, Richard Drew 1989.
James Kelman, *Not Not While the Giro*, Polygon 1983.
The Burn, Secker and Warburg 1991.
Jessie Kesson, *Where the Apple Ripens*, Hogarth 1986.
Glitter of Mica, Hogarth 1987.
Eric Linklater, *The Stories of Eric Linklater*, Macmillan 1968.
William McIlvanney, *Walking Wounded*, Hodder 1989.
Iain Crichton Smith, *Selected Stories*, Constable 1990.
Muriel Spark, *Collected Stories*, Macmillan 1967.
The Go-Away Bird and Other Stories, Penguin 1984.
Alan Spence, *Its Colours They Are Fine*, Collins 1977, Corgi 1987.
David Toulmin, *Hard Shining Corn*, Impulse 1972.
Straw into Gold, Gourdas House 1981. *Chiel Amang Them*, Gourdas
  House 1982.
Fred Urquhart, *Full Score*, Aberdeen University Press 1989.
Duncan Williamson, *Fireside Tales of the Traveller Children*, Canongate
  1985.
May the Devil Walk Behind Ye!, Canongate 1989.